THE RICH AND
THE DAMNED

Also By Richard Himmel

Beyond Desire
The Sharp Edge

The Johnny Maguire Series

I'll Find You
The Chinese Keyhole
I Have Gloria Kirby
Two Deaths Must Die
The Rich and the Damned

THE RICH AND THE DAMNED

RICHARD HIMMEL

CUTTING EDGE

ISBN-13: 978-1-952138-26-3

Published by
Cutting Edge Publishing
PO Box 8212
Calabasas, CA 91372
www.cuttingedgebooks.com

CHAPTER ONE

IT WAS an old fortress of a house, a brownstone mansion with turrets and towers, a battlemented edge running around the roof. It was a castle kids dream of building but gooped-up by the fancy hand of a Victorian architect and weathered now, decayed and rotted by eighty years of Chicago wind, rain and sleet. I was looking at it over my shoulder as I paid off the cab driver. I over-tipped in view of the neighborhood I was in, made the turn, opened the big iron gate and started the long walk to the front door. I had a lot of time to think about whether or not to use the front door. I was straight with myself; I knew I was out of my league here, outclassed. The Prince of Wales had used this front door. Presidents had used the front door. Tycoons, moguls and society dolls used the front door. My gray flannel suit and brand-new attaché case wouldn't fool anyone. I was strictly a night-school lawyer from the wrong side of town, and not so long ago if someone had mentioned narrow lapels I would have thought it was a horse in the third race at Arlington.

Now I touched my narrow lapels, felt the inside pocket to make sure the telegram was there. It was there, all right, and inside that dilapidated castle was the woman who had sent it to me.

Once this woman had said to me, "I know you, Maguire. I know what you are. You're a big man, aren't you, a tough guy? You've got muscles where other men never thought of having muscles. And you have a steel jaw and an iron gut." She punched hard and fast against my naked stomach. Then she smiled at me in the funny way she has of smiling. "Big man," she repeated, "but you know what? You've got big, soft gray eyes like a puppy dog." She put her fingers against my lips, held them there. "And a mouth as soft as a baby's rear end."

My mouth moved wetly against her fingers as I talked. "So what? So what does it mean?"

"It means as tough as you are and as big as you are, when I whistle, you and those puppy dog eyes will come running and all that iron and steel will be so much jelly."

Like a puppy dog, I snapped at her fingers, caught them between my teeth. I bit hard. Her knee came up and expertly jabbed me. I let go quick, cursed out loud. She threw her head back and laughed. It was as close as I had been in a long time to being in love.

The telegram in my pocket was the whistle, and here I was puppy-dogging it to the front door. Halfway up the walk, I saw a hearse pull around from the rear of the house, a long gray-and-black job, loaded with chrome glistening in the late afternoon sun. The car stopped near a portico at the side entrance. The chauffeur jumped out, opened the back door, stood at attention, waiting. I avoided the front door, cut across the lawn, walked over to the hearse. "Somebody die?"

"I ain't delivering groceries," he dead-panned, looking straight ahead.

I stood in front of him. "All right, clown. Let's have it straight. Who died?"

"How should I know? You can't tell with these rich ones. Maybe it's some old lady's pet canary."

Kibitzing this wiseacre would get me nowhere. The side door was open. It was a compromise between the front door and back door, just about where I belonged. I rang the bell there and waited. I rang again, but still got no action. The door was unlocked so I walked in, through the dark, narrow passage and into a large, square reception hall with a marble floor that echoed under my footsteps.

Since making my way in the world I had rubbed my nose in some elegant layouts, but this was the most. A couple of iron gates and it would have made a hell of a railroad station. There were voices coming from upstairs. I turned around. The staircase was wide and fancy, all carpeted in dark red. At the landing was a tremendous stained-glass window, like in a church. It was a hell of a setup for a hungover Sunday morning; fall out of bed, down a few stairs, say a fast prayer and crawl back up to sleep it off.

A procession started down the stairs. First a dark-suited man, gray-gloved, and with a dark hat in hand. Following him were two gray-uniformed attendants struggling with the weight inside a wicker casket. Then another dark-suited man, twin to the first.

"For God's sakes be careful with that thing. Can't you handle your job? Don't you know what you're doing?" I turned around, looked higher up. She was leaning over the railing. The sunlight through the stained-glass window caught her hair just right, put it on fire. This was no ordinary red hair. This was not the carrot-top variety that my relatives have. This was the red the leaves turn at the end of autumn—rich red, like that. She went right on hollering. "And be careful of that damn window. You're going to back right into it." All the way down she was shouting directions at them, heckling them, giving them hell.

When they were safely on the marble floor, they set down the casket and caught their breath. One of them started to take a handkerchief to wipe his brow, but the dark-suited man touted him off with a frown. She zipped down the stairs then, carelessly, as though she had done it thousands of times before. "I'd hate to see you men try to move a piano."

She saw me then, stopped for a moment, then went on. "Hello, Maguire. How the hell did you get in?" I was set to face her and say the words I had ready to say, but she kept walking, passing me by, following the casket as the men edged it through the narrow passage and out the side door. She waited until the casket was in the hearse and the door of the car was closed. She turned around, kicked the door shut and came back into the reception hall.

She was dressed in narrow gray pants, a man's white shirt opened at the throat. Her head was down and the tip of her long thumbnail was between her teeth. She was in front of me, but she didn't look up and she didn't say anything. With a cat's swiftness she wheeled around and shouted up the stairs. "Mr. Pritchard! Mr. Pritchard! Come down here, please. We are pressed for time and there is much to be done." Still without looking up, she said, "I suppose if undertakers were bright they wouldn't be undertakers." Before I had a chance to say anything she shouted up the stairs again. "Mr. Pritchard, what's taking you so long?"

He appeared finally, another dark-suited man, more elegantly dressed. His expression of professional compassion was loused up by the lines of anguish around his eyes and mouth. "This is all so terribly irregular, Miss Donnelly," he complained.

"Come on now, Mr. Pritchard. You've had crises before. The undertaking business must be like any other business. You have to be prepared for the unexpected. Now let's get these arrangements settled." She paused, made a flourish with her hand. "Take notes, Mr. Pritchard. In your condition you probably won't remember anything." She waited until he pulled a small black book from his pocket, clicked his Papermate into action. "Don't look so unhappy, Mr. Pritchard. Eventually there will be a lovely, expensive funeral. We won't miss a trick, I promise you that."

"There are certain formalities, Miss Donnelly."

"Damn the formalities and do as I say. The most important thing is not to bring him back here until I give the all-clear. Fix him up or do whatever hocus-pocus you do but don't bring him back here until I call you."

"I understand."

"And no one is to know who the body is. No one. Make up a fictitious name. If they connect him with this house say it's the butler or the chauffeur. No one must know who it is. Avoid the newspapers and radio people completely."

"About the casket, Miss Donnelly?"

"The best. But you damn well better not try to rob me, Mr. Pritchard. I'll compare prices later."

"Any other special requests when the body is brought back here?"

She put both hands to her head. "Oh, my God, I suppose there ought to be a wake."

Mr. Pritchard's Protestant ears perked up. "A wake?"

"Yes, a wake. He was born a Catholic. I suppose there ought to be a wake. I don't know one damn thing about wakes. I'm not strong enough for a wake." She wheeled around quickly. "Hey, Maguire, you ought to know something about wakes."

"Sure I do. What do you want to know?"

"The hell with it. He hadn't been in a church for twenty-five years. It'll be too much trouble, besides everything else. Forget it. I've made up my mind there will definitely not be a wake. You take care of the flowers, don't you, Mr. Pitchard?"

"We can."

"Then do it." She paced in a circle. "I guess that's everything. You can run along now, Mr. Pritchard. I'll call you later."

The funeral director put his book and pen away. "Let me say again, Miss Donnelly, how sorry I am."

She stopped, looked over at him. For a minute she was not the woman running on a rotary edge of nerves. Her eyes glistened, her voice was softer, lower, coming from deep inside. "Sorry, Mr. Pritchard? You don't know what sorry is." In a quick movement she started up the stairs, but remembered me as an afterthought. "Come with me, Maguire." She ran fast and I walked slowly. She left the door of a room open, I followed her inside and closed the door behind me.

❧   ❧   ❧

The room had been a bedroom once but was now converted into an office. Steel files were stacked against flowered wallpaper. Electric computing machines were lined up on a carved railing of golden oak. The place looked ransacked. Papers were hanging out of file drawers. Stacks of files were strewn on the floor. The vault door was open and documentary debris spilled from it.

She was curled up on a window seat in the bay window, looking out across the lawn. "Now, listen, Maguire, we might as well understand each other from the beginning."

I dropped my attaché case, took off my jacket, loosened my tie and rolled up my sleeves. "First say hello to me, Red."

"I'm sorry. I'm upset. There has been so much confusion."

I walked over to her, took her chin in my hand, turned her face so that she had to look at me. Wonderful green eyes, hot and cold at once, fire and ice. "Say it, Red."

She whispered the words. "Hello, Maguire."

"Now you kiss me." She stiffened as I put my mouth against hers, tensed up, ready to fight me off. But it was a quick kiss with nothing behind it. "Now, you say something like 'long time no see.'"

"It has been a long time," she said. "I've missed you, Maguire. I didn't know it until this minute, but I've missed you."

"Me, too, Red. Miss you hard."

"Look, let's get this straight. This is not like the other times. This is business."

I smiled. "We've had business before."

"Don't be vulgar."

"I meant to be cute."

"You're not the type," she snapped. "I can't talk to you unless you agree to my terms. Straight business. Agreed?"

I sat down beside her. "Not so fast. I can't be had so easy. State your business."

"It's a long story. I'm not sure how to begin."

"First tell me who died."

She hesitated, looked out the window, fought the battle to keep controlled. "My father," she said.

"Oh, Red, I'm sorry. I didn't know. I had no idea."

"Everyone has to die. He was sick and he died. That's all."

"No it isn't all," I said. "I know how much he meant to you. I know how close you two were."

"Stop it, Maguire."

I understood everything then, the reason for her being the way she was, the naily exterior and the harsh words. "Have you cried yet, Red? Here, let me look at you." I took her face in my hands, made her look at me again. "No, you haven't cried. You've been a big, strong girl and haven't cried." I could see the tears beginning. "You ought to cry, Red. You loved him and he was everything to you. Go ahead and cry, cry your heart out."

She bit back the tears, tried to shake free of me. "Stop it!"

"You're human, Red. Let yourself cry. You'll feel better. Come on." She reached around and bit my hand. I let go and then slapped her across the face. She cried out and began to cry then, not a slow beginning of tears but at a full pitch of sadness. I took her into my arms and held her, hard. She let it all out, all her sadness. She cried with her whole being, loud and raging. I held her tighter, letting my body absorb the shock of her grief and taking the impact of her fingernails digging through my shirt into my back and feeling the wetness of her tears against my face. Gradually the pace of her crying began to subside, the shaking of her body stilled and after a few minutes the tears were spent, flushed out in a flash flood. "Damn you, Maguire." She took my handkerchief. "I promised myself that I wouldn't cry."

"You'll feel better now."

"Will I? A lot you know. A lot anyone knows. You never knew my father, never knew the man he really was."

Carleton Donnelly was famous for being one of the biggest bastards in the country. He was one of the last tycoons, a die-hard autocrat in an increasing democracy. His name and his dough backed up every cause dedicated to making the big man bigger and the small man smaller. He was antilabor, antiliberal, antiprogressive. He ran an empire of steel mills, lumber camps, oil lands, mines, and everything else he could lay his moneyed hands on. And his moneyed hands weren't so clean. The beginning of this empire was not his, it belonged to his father-in-law, Simon Forrester. In his day Simon Forrester was a civic leader, a revered man, a founding father, a great philanthropist. This was Forrester's house, and all the things which Donnelly controlled were projects Forrester had started.

This family was a Chicago legend, front-page copy, financial page news and society column notes for the last eighty years. A kid growing up in Chicago knew the Forrester story the way he knew about Washington and Lincoln. It started with a dry-goods store that grew into Forrester's department store which expanded into a chain of department stores. Money makes money and old Simon Forrester had the knack for it. First lumber, and through lumber, paper. Then newspapers, then oil, then mines, then steel. He made it big and socked it away before taxes were around to bite off the big chunks. Even wasteland real estate hanging dead for years yielded valuable minerals when the time was right.

Simon Forrester had one child, a daughter. His wife had died producing this daughter. Dolly Forrester grew up in this house, pampered and spoiled and adored by everyone. While she was visiting relatives in Atlanta she met, fell in love and eloped with Carleton Donnelly. She came home with her husband and equipped with her husband's two small children. The marriage broke Simon Forrester's heart, and it came finally to break his spirit. Year by year the unwelcome son-in-law, by working from within, began to take the power of the Forrester Industries away from the old man. Donnelly was a big man, vital and powerful, smart as a whip. He managed, mismanaged, connived and cheated until he had his hands on everything he wanted. Simon Forrester gave up, finally; there was no reason to fight. He lived out his days an old man on a bench in Lincoln Park, feeding pigeons, still idolizing his daughter and cursing the day he had sent her to Atlanta.

This woman was Rourke Donnelly, the child of Carleton Donnelly's first wife. The other child of Carleton Donnelly's who came to live in the Forrester house was Russell, a no-good bum who made front pages and gossip columns. Then there were the two children Donnelly had with Dolly Forrester, a tepid boy and a pale girl who never made the newspapers except for an occasional polite notice on the society page.

I was honest with myself. I was not in love with Rourke Donnelly. I looked at her in her sadness and felt sorry for her. I looked at her beauty, the tight quick way she moved her body, and I wanted her. But I wasn't in love with her, maybe because I wouldn't let myself be. It was an accident that I even knew her. We lived only a couple of miles apart, but I was nowhere near her league. I met her two summers before, in July.

The law business is slow in July; courts are closed and, let's face it, I don't have a hell of a practice anyway. A guy I know has a cabin on a lake in northern Wisconsin. He gave me the key, told me where he kept the fishing tackle, and I took off for a few days of fresh air and seclusion.

It wasn't a very big lake but it was big enough, and there weren't many fish but there was enough action to keep me interested. I was fishing late one night, later than usual. The walleyes were hitting, and I stayed out to take advantage of it. A storm came up suddenly, a big wind and bolts of lightning zigzagging through the storm-clouded sky. I like electric storms. They do something to me—I feel scared and brave all at once. They turn a lot of inside machinery into motion, make me feel horny.

I would have stayed out in the storm, but the first bolt of lightning sent the walleyes down to the bottom and it was hard handling both the line and the boat in the rough water. I started up the outboard and cut across the lake toward my cabin. It was blowing hard, controlling the boat was tricky through the rocky water. As I skirted a little island I saw another boat in trouble; a big boulder stuck out from the water and the wind was pummeling the little boat against it. I changed course and steered over. As I came close, one big wave slapped the other boat hard against the boulder. There was the sound of splintering wood. The boat disintegrated and left a figure struggling in the water. I grabbed an outstretched arm and pulled the figure aboard. It was Rourke Donnelly, as scared as anyone can be, and wet through. She crouched on the deck, clinging to a seat, her whole body shaking. There was no time to do anything about her. I had to get my own boat the hell out of there before it, too, was reduced to matchsticks. I headed straight across the water, docked the boat, lashed it to the pier, picked her up and carried her into my cabin.

She could have been anybody. I didn't know who she was and I didn't care. She was a woman and she. was cold and wet and scared. She clung to me for her life. Like I said, electrical storms do crazy things to me. It was that kind of night. Wordless and alive. The pounding thunder and crackling lightning were counterpoint music to the music of loving.

She stayed with me that whole week. We didn't talk very much or ask any questions. It was enough that we were together. She would not tell me her name. I figured she was married so I let it pass and called her Red. When it came time to leave, she said, "I'll meet you here the first Friday in October." And that's the way it was. Once, during the winter which followed, my doorbell rang in the middle of the night. She came into my apartment without a word. I don't know how she found me, there are maybe twelve John Patrick Maguires in the telephone directory. But there she was and there was no need for words. When it was over she kissed me and said, "I'll see you June twenty-fourth." We spent that week in June together and met again in October. Twice during that winter she came to my apartment unexpectedly. Once I had another girl in the bedroom but she didn't seem to mind and I finished out the night with her in the living room.

Now spring was beginning again.

"I know what people thought of him," she was saying. "I know how everyone hated my father. They were afraid of him, afraid of his power and afraid of his brains and vitality. They didn't understand him. You might have understood him, Maguire. You would have liked him if you had known him. He was tough, like you, and yet he could be gentle. He was your size and your build. But he was smarter than you, a lot smarter. He thought big, he acted big." She studied me for a moment, seeing me and seeing her father. "Why aren't you more than you are, Maguire?"

I laughed. "What the hell am I supposed to be, head of the Board of Trade? I think I did pretty well, all things considered. My mother went out and did rich people's washing. My father was a bricklayer who got stewed every payday. Sound familiar? I'm a back-of-the-yards boy. Until I was ten years old I thought everything was supposed to smell the way it does at the stock yards. My boyhood friends are either hoodlums or bricklayers getting stewed every payday. I got to be a lawyer, Red, a genuine counselor-at-law, and I did it all by myself without stepping on anybody and without owing one person in the world one thing. Maybe that's why I'm not more than I am. I never stepped on anybody and I'm not beholden to anybody. It's a good feeling."

"You've had chances to be big. Why haven't you grabbed them?"

"What chances?"

"Dino Sloan," she said.

"How do you know about him?"

"I know a lot about you, Maguire. In one of those file cabinets is a complete dossier on John Patrick Maguire. I know how much rent you pay, I know how much money you make. I know that you sleep with the girl who runs the secretarial answering service in your office building."

"You do, huh? Do you know how many nights a week?"

"It depends," she answered, "on your other interests at the moment."

There was a studio couch. I lay down there, kicked off my shoes, and stared at the ceiling. "Who told you about Dino Sloan?"

"Why didn't you take his offer? You could have made a lot of money and moved up from him into the big time. There are other men like Sloan. You could have had them all, named your own fees. Then, once you were established and successful, you could have gone out after a respectable practice."

"Dino Sloan is a bum. All his pals are bums. I'd rather be a bricklayer than a lawyer to those slobs."

"Noble, Maguire, but stupid."

"Okay, so I'm stupid."

She came over to the couch, sat on the edge, put her hand on my foot and massaged it gently. "What would you say if I offered you a job?"

"I couldn't take money for doing anything I enjoy that much."

She pinched my foot so that it hurt. "I'm serious. I'm asking to retain your services."

"As what? Chief legal counsel to the Forrester Industries? I'm just the boy, got just the background."

She spoke slowly now; the words were hard for her to get out. "I need help, Maguire. I need your kind of help. I need you."

I crossed my legs so that she could massage the other foot. "You know, Red, people have come to me before saying they need help. But it has very little to do with legal services. The word has gotten around that I have a thick skull that's hard to crack and that I have a strong arm and know how to use a gun. It hurts my pride. I'm not such a bad lawyer, you know."

"I need someone I can trust." She crawled up on the couch and lay beside me, her head in the crook of my arm. "Listen to me, now, and listen hard. I have a superhuman job to do, and I can't do it alone. I have no one else to turn to; you have to help me. You can't ask any questions. You have to do as I ask and do it on trust. I need you, Maguire. Those words are hard for me to say but I need you."

"What about your brothers?"

She spit out laughter. "What about them? A great pair of men they are. They should be here now, shouldn't they? The bereaved sons should be here doing what I'm doing, taking charge. But where are they? My brother Russell could be anywhere. He could be in Africa or China—or Hollywood or Alaska. He could be on a yacht in the Mediterranean. He could even be in a flophouse right here on West Madison Street. But I don't know where he is and I have to find him. I have to find him at once. He has to be here before the secret gets out that my father is dead."

"Why the secret?"

"Business reasons—and remember, no questions, blind trust."

I rubbed my cheek against her hair. "I haven't agreed to anything yet." Her hair smelled good. "What about your other brother?"

"Young Forrester? He's a prize. He's the family scholar, you know. He's a scholar only because he doesn't have the guts to be anything more active. Young Forrester is supposed to be in Boston at an institution of higher learning, but he isn't there today. I've talked to everyone including the damn president of the university, and they can't find him. They've swept out the library and he isn't there. Someone thinks he may have gone to Washington. I have our Washington man on it. If Forrester is in Washington, we'll find him."

"What do you have, your own private gestapo?"

"Will you help me, Maguire?"

I sat up, moved out of her touch, walked over to the window seat and looked out on the traffic. It was like any afternoon in Chicago, the rush hour beginning, the smells of buses releasing their stinking diesel fumes. I should have been in Tina Weston's office, signing the letters I had dictated earlier that day and making small talk with Tina.

"Red, I have to ask questions."

"I don't have to answer them."

"Your father dies and you have to keep it a secret. This room gets torn up because something is missing. It could be dough, it could be documents, it could be a will. But something is missing, something important, and that's one reason to keep it a secret. You need your brothers here for a reason—not the reasons you said. You'll run the show no matter what. You've got a big master plot in your head and you've got a lot of little pieces to juggle to bring it off. This is a big plot. You're like your father, aren't you? You think big and you act big. So you have all these pieces to juggle and you need a boy to run strong-arm errands for you. That's me. What does the dossier say? Honest, reliable, dumb ..."

"Will you do it, Maguire?"

"You know, Red, it could be worse. You could lie to me. You could say you love me and get me to do it for love. You could say it's straight legal work and you want to give me a break."

"Will you do it, Maguire?"

There was no use thinking about it. "Who do I kill first?"

"You find my brother Russell."

"A needle in an international haystack?"

"I have two leads. First of all I had better explain that technically ... at least I think it's technically, Russell has been disowned, disinherited. He disgraced the family once too often, and my father forbade any of us to ever see him or to be in contact with him. But I've read gossip columns and know there are rumors about him and that blonde movie star who's old enough to be his mother. Clarice Cabot. I called Miss Cabot to see if she had Russ tucked in with her. She says his picture doesn't start until next week. He isn't due out until then. Can you imagine what that damn fool is doing in the movies? He has no more talent than a window shade. But you know what will happen? The female population will take one look at those soulful eyes, that slow smiling mouth and there will be a nation in love with him. If the producers are smart enough they'll expose him bare-chested and there will be panic in the streets. Up to now this is the history of my brother on a limited scale. Hollywood means he can seduce them by the millions, and all the time dragging the family name down with him. This is simply wonderful for the prestige of the Forrester Industries."

"Well, if he's due in Hollywood next week, chances are he's in this country now. He can't be too far away. What about your gestapo?"

"Mary is the answer," Rourke said. "Sweet, innocent Mary is the answer. Mary is the baby of the family. She's twenty-three years old and I don't think has ever been kissed. I'll brief you quickly on Mary. She's a sallow-faced child who combines all the worst Forrester features and not one damn Donnelly characteristic, good or bad. Mary is the defenseless type; she must be protected. I have a red-hot suspicion that darling brother Russ keeps an eye on Mary. He worries about her, worries that Father and I mistreat her. If she were in trouble she would go only to him, and to go to him she would have to know where he is. I am certain that they somehow correspond secretly. Mary will never tell me where Russ is in a million years, but she will probably tell you."

"Why me? She doesn't even know me."

"You're a man, Maguire, and you look protective. And you're honest. Honesty oozes out of you. Mary is just simple enough to be a sucker for your kind of open-faced honesty. And you're attractive. No man looks twice at Mary. If you look twice, you'll have clear sailing."

"Where do I find Mary?" I sat down, put on my shoes.

"At the end of the hall. Her door is locked. You'll have to spirit your way in. She lets no one in her inner sanctum." I rolled down my sleeves, put on my coat. "We'd better get it clear about money," Rourke said. "There's a thousand dollars of expense money in that envelope. Take it. It's only the beginning. Spend what you need to accomplish the results."

I picked up the envelope, weighed it in my hand, then put it in my pocket. "I don't know you very well, Red. I know where the mole is on your back and I can close my eyes and feel how your skin is when I touch you. But I don't know anything about you."

"It's not important."

"Where is it all going to lead, Red? Murder, rape, robbery?"

"Find Russell," she said.

"You're after blood. I don't know whose blood, but I'm glad I'm on your side."

"On my side all the way?" she asked.

"Until I see a danger signal." I walked to the door. "Is Mary's room at the end of the hall to the right or left?"

"To the right."

"Come here, Red."

"What for?" she asked, but she knew the answer, kissed me.

CHAPTER TWO

KNOCKED twice and waited each time, but there was no answer. She was moving around inside but she wouldn't answer the door. I knocked again with my whole fist. A small, thin voice came through the door. "I won't come out, Rourke, and I won't let you in. It's no use. You can't make me."

"It isn't Rourke," I said.

"Who is it?"

I started to say that I was a friend of Rourke's, but decided against it. "You don't know me, Mary. My name is John Maguire."

"What do you want?"

"I want to talk to you."

"What about?"

"I want to discuss something with you, Mary. I'm a lawyer."

"Is it about the will?"

"Partially," I answered. "Come on, now, open the door."

"Do you swear you're alone?" she asked. "Promise that Rourke isn't with you? Cross your heart?"

"I am alone, Mary."

"Cross your heart?"

I crossed my heart. "Cross my heart," I said and felt like a damn fool playing children's games in the deserted hallway.

"If it's about the will, I guess it's all right. I'll unlock the door but you mustn't come in right away. I look awful. Count to fifteen before you come in so I can comb my hair. Promise?"

"I promise." The key turned in the lock. Slowly, like a conscientious boy playing hide-and-seek, I counted to fifteen, opened the door and went into the room. It was empty. There was the sound of running water behind a closed door.

Once this had been a beautiful room. It had been pink and blue and white, ruffled and frilly the way a little girl's room should be. Age, decay and neglect had turned it into a ghoulish horror. The lace curtains at the window were yellow and threadbare in places. The birds and flowers of the wallpaper were almost indistinguishable now, faded out and trapped in a network of plaster cracks. There was a chair and some kind of sofa deal loaded with French dolls. I picked one up; dust flew from it and the delicate fabric skirt cracked under the pressure of my hand. I felt as if I was in a room which had been closed up for fifty years. There was no sign of life, only of death and dying.

When Mary made her entrance from the bathroom, I didn't know whether to laugh or cry for her. Rourke had told me she was a plain-looking girl. But this afternoon, behind her locked door, she had painted over the plainness, veneered the girl she was into her own conception of glamour. Her face was masked expressionless with a thick white greasepaint which did not quite hide the blemishes of her skin. Her lips were painted bright red, thicker than they really were. Her eyes were rimmed with carefully penciled black lines and some greenish stuff was smeared over her lids. Her mouse-colored hair was pulled slick back and ended on her neck with a bunch of curls going in all directions. She was dressed in a shiny black dress, cut too low in front and fancied up with some black organdy business going down the side. This was a plain girl burlesquing beauty, a burlesque of the kind of beauty Rourke has.

"Hello, Mary. I'm John Maguire."

She looked at me closely, squinting a little, as if she was used to wearing glasses. "You couldn't be one of Father's lawyers. You're much too good-looking to be one of Father's lawyers. They are either old, terrible men or those pimply-faced young ones." She made a vague gesture. "Please sit down. What do you want to talk about?" She saw that I was searching for a clear area to park in. With one sweep she brushed all the dolls off the settee. They fell in a cloud of dust to the floor. "I'm busting to talk to someone. I saw them carry Father out. I watched from the window; I overlook the driveway. There was such an attractive man driving the hearse. He saw me watching and flirted with me. Isn't that awful? He flirted with me."

"Mary," I began. "It is all right to call you Mary, isn't it?"

"Of course it is. Call me Mary. You make it sound like such a wonderful name."

"Mary, I'm sorry about your father."

"Are you? I'm not. I've been expecting it. They haven't been able to keep the secret from me. Maybe they fooled everyone else, but they didn't fool me. I knew he was dying. They tried so hard to keep the secret. Business reasons. Everything Father and Rourke do is for business reasons. You know Rourke never even told me that Father died. She didn't call me to his bedside when he took his final breath. I always dreamed of what would happen when he died. He would call me to his bedside and I would kneel beside him and he would put a feeble hand on my hair and tell me how sorry he was for the way he treated me all my life and tell me that he loved me and that he didn't mean to be so horrid to me. And I would hold his hand and forgive him. At least part of the time I dreamed I forgave him. The other times I laughed in his face."

"Maybe there wasn't time to call you when he died."

She shook her head sadly. "There was a lot of time. He died last night. I was listening outside the door. Rourke was locked in with him. I heard her scream when he died." She rubbed her hands over her bare arms. "It gives me goose bumps when I remember the scream. She stayed locked in with him all night. Isn't that eerie, being locked up with a dead man all night? I can't stand to see dead people. When Grandpa Forrester died they brought him back here and they made me go down to the parlor to see him. I didn't want to go. I cried, but it didn't matter. Father said I had to go and I went. I saw poor Grandpa Forrester dead in his coffin and I got sick to my stomach and up-chucked all over the rug Father had brought back from China. The spot is still there. They could never properly get it out. Father was so angry. He was fond of the rug. It was no good trying to explain how I felt. Rourke and Father never know how other people feel, only how *they* feel. I would have died of shame—killed myself if it hadn't been for my brother Russell. My brother Russell is such a lovely boy. Do you know him?"

"No," I said, "but it's about Russell that I wanted to see you. Do you know where he is?"

She closed up then, drew herself in. "So that's it. Rourke sent you to find out if I know where Russ is. Well, I don't know and you can tell Rourke that even if I did know I wouldn't tell her. Or you. Father forbade us ever to see Russell or to write to him. Father forbade so many things." She stopped pacing the room, got on her hands and knees, reached under the bed and came up with a package of cigarettes and an ashtray. "Just think, I can smoke now whenever I please. I don't have to be afraid of what Father will say. It was always all right for Rourke to smoke, but not Mary. He didn't have morals about smoking but he always said smoking did not become me. Nothing was becoming to me, according to Father. I didn't look good in make-up or in pretty dresses, so I had to go around drab-looking. My father was a horrid man, Mr. Maguire. He was horrid to everybody except Rourke. He didn't love my mother; he only married her to get Grandpa Forrester's money. Poor Grandpa Forrester. My father hated everyone but Rourke." She squinted at me. "It isn't a pretty story with a happy ending, is it, Mr. Maguire? We're not pretty people, none of us. We could have been. We have everything to be pretty with. All the money, this wonderful house. I have never enjoyed one minute since I was born. I tried to escape. I could have been married. There were boys who wanted to marry me. Maybe they weren't handsome or bright or wonderful, but some of them were nice boys. My father said they didn't want me, they only wanted the Forrester money. I suppose that was true. Who would want me, just me? I wouldn't have cared, though. I've been so damn lonely." She had been smoking in quick, short, awkward puffs. Now she had begun to cry, the tears staining her make-up, running the black stuff around her eyes. But she went on talking, not aware that she was crying. "It will be different now. Now that Father is dead everything will be different. I hope it isn't too late. It can't be too late. I'll have all that money now in my own name. Have you seen the will? Did Rourke find it?"

"I don't know."

"You said you came about the will."

"Mary, I had to get in to see you. I have to find your brother."

She wasn't even listening. "You're a lawyer, Mr. Maguire. Even if he didn't leave me anything in his will, I have a legal right to my share, don't I? I mean he had no reason to cut me off. It wasn't even his money. I mean it's Forrester money and Sonny and I are the only ones with Forrester blood. The courts would understand that, wouldn't they?"

"Mary, I don't know anything about the will."

Her tears changed to laughter. "Neither does Rourke. Isn't that a scream? Rourke doesn't know what's in the will. I watched through the keyhole while she tore the room apart. She's had every lawyer on the phone. Wouldn't it be funny if there is no will? What if he died and left no will? I would surely get my share then, wouldn't I?"

"Yes."

"It'll be different now. I'll be the kind of woman men like. I'll dress beautifully. I bought this dress because I knew he was dying. I took an awful chance. It was so expensive. I charged it and hoped he would be dead before the first of the month when the bill came in. I bought it because it was black and no matter how I feel I will have to be in mourning. There will be so many people coming here and I will have to look nice." She stood up, twirled around. "I do look nice, don't I, Mr. Maguire? This dress is becoming, isn't it?" She stopped at a long, narrow gilt mirror. "Isn't it?" she said into the mirror. "Don't I look nice?"

I tried to lie to her, but no words would come out.

Mary wheeled around, came up to me, knelt in front of me, crying harder now. "I like you, Maguire, because you're not a liar. You're an honest man. I like you just fine." She jumped up, examining herself in the mirror again. "I don't look nice; I look horrid. This dress is terrible." She ripped at the organdy ruffle. "My face looks like a Halloween mask. It's terrible to be plain-looking. Everyone is polite and says I look like my mother. It's not true. Her eyes were bluer and her hair was blonder and her skin was clearer and her hands were more delicate and she was lovely." She rubbed her hands over her face, the wet tears blurring the red and green and black of her make-up into a mess. "Everything that was beautiful in Mother got mixed up with the Donnelly blood and came out ugly in me." She stopped suddenly, put her hand over her mouth and rushed for the bathroom.

I heard the toilet seat go up and the retching sound begin. I remembered all the times when I have gone over my quota of Irish whisky and longed for a cool hand on my hot head. I followed her into the bathroom, held her head as she vomited. When she stopped being sick, I sat her down on the toilet seat, wet a wash rag with hot water, soaped it well and scrubbed her face until it was shining clean. I handed her a comb and smiled at her as she loosened the bouquet of curls and combed her hair so that it fell straight and easy to her shoulders.

"Now you look like something," I said.

She smiled, reached for her glasses on the sink. "I suppose I should be ashamed or embarrassed. You've seen me at my absolute worst. But I don't feel that way with you."

"My Irish mother had a great remedy for all human ills—a good cry and a healthy bowel movement. You've accomplished the same thing and you ought to feel like a million bucks."

"You're sweet to bother with me."

"I think we're going to be great friends, Mary."

Her smile changed to sadness. "I guess I'm destined to have friends, and no lovers." She stood up. "Well, it doesn't matter. I was foolish to try to be anything else but what I am. It doesn't matter. I'll have money and freedom. I'll travel a lot. Maybe I'll meet a nice man. I hope he looks like you but it won't matter what he looks like. He'll want to marry me. I'll know the reason. He'll be after my money but I'll pretend I don't know that. I'll be very careful that he's a nice man, sweet and gentle, a man who likes children."

"You don't have to rush into anything."

"It won't matter that he marries me for my money. Once we're married, I'll make him fall in love with me. I'll know how to treat a man, to take care of him, make him want me. I've thought about this for a long time and I'll know exactly what to do."

"He'll be a lucky guy, Mary."

She patted my face. "I think maybe he will. Now, why don't you go back to Rourke. I think I need time to lick my wounds."

"What about Russell?"

"Tell Rourke I don't know where he is … No, wait. Don't lie to her. I know where to find him. But tell Rourke I won't tell, she'll never get it out of me."

"Mary, let me explain something to you. Your father is dead. He was an important man to the world. No matter what kind of man he was to his children he was important to the world. This isn't just an ordinary man dying. You have to understand that. Try to see some of this from Rourke's point of view. She has to make all the arrangements, run the whole show."

"But that's what Rourke likes to do—make all the arrangements, run the whole show."

"I don't pretend to understand Rourke, Mary. She's brewing a plot. I don't know what it is or what it involves. I've told her I'd help her if I could. For some reason she thinks all the children should be here together. She thinks it's vitally important.

She needs Russell and she can't find him. Your brother cannot be hurt now, Mary. Your father is dead. He can't hurt Russell anymore." I was giving this last bit everything I had, the whole trusted-family-friend routine. "It's important that he be here now not only for appearances, but for legal reasons."

"You mean about the will?"

"Yes."

She laughed. "He won't get a dime. Father hated him worse than any of us. He hated Russell because Russell looked like him and could have been like him but wasn't. Russ is nice. That's why he hated Russ the most."

"Tell me where he is, Mary."

"I don't know. That's the truth. The last time I heard from him he was on somebody's yacht. I had a perfectly lovely letter from Algiers. He writes to me at a friend's house, keeps me posted that way. He was having a lovely time on the yacht. So romantic. If I were a man I would like to be Russell."

"You love him very much, don't you?"

"More than anything. All my life he's looked after me, took my side against the others."

"Mary, I'll make you a deal. You tell me how to find Russell, and I promise I won't tell Rourke. I'll find Russell myself. I'll tell him what's happened. If he wants to come home, I'll bring him back. If he doesn't, I'll leave him alone and never tell Rourke I found him. How's that?"

"But you're Rourke's friend. How can I trust you?"

"I'm your friend, too."

"I suppose he should know that Father is dead. He won't care. He won't be glad the way I am. He just won't care."

"He has a right to know, a right to decide for himself whether he'll come home or not."

She had her finger in her mouth, sucking at it. "I don't know what to do. If I only could trust you. Will you swear it on the Bible?"

"We don't have to get dramatic about this thing. I give you my word."

"It has to be on the Bible." She took the book from under her night table. "This is my mother's Bible. Swear on it and I'll tell you how to find Russ."

I was wishing I was back in the old neighborhood where a man wouldn't be caught dead swearing on a Bible unless he was in a courtroom. But I had one thousand cold dollars in my pocket, a vague uneasiness in my innards and an increasing interest in the Forrester-Donnelly clan. I put my hand on the Bible and said what she wanted me to say, and for no reason at all was thinking about my mother.

"You know how serious it is to swear on the Bible, don't you?" I nodded. "In the letter from Algiers, Russ said he was coming back. I thought I'd hear from him a week ago, but I haven't. He said if I ever get into any trouble and need him for help, I should contact a man named Edward Furst. He said I could find him through a bar on Rush Street. The bar is called Singapore Sling. He said the man there would always know where to find him."

It wasn't much to go on. Russell Donnelly could be anywhere between Algiers and Hollywood. But it was a start. "Thank you, Mary."

"Will you be back here?"

"Yes."

"Tell me what you find out." As I started to leave she put her hand on my arm. "Tell me something. Are you a special friend of Rourke's? You seem different from the others. Are you in love with her, too?"

"There are lots of more important things to think about, Mary. I wouldn't bother thinking about love."

Rourke was in the converted office, talking on the phone. "I don't give a damn if it is after hours and there are three time locks and twenty combinations. Get that safety deposit box the hell over here. What's the point of owning a bank if you can't get special service." She hung up, turned in the swivel chair. "Holy cow, I wonder if I'll ever get through this."

"Through what?"

"This mess."

"You look capable."

"Damn right I'm capable, but I have bigger things to do than planning a funeral. How did you make out with Mary?"

I saw the Bible, felt the leather binding against my hand. "I got nowhere with Mary," I said. "Where do you keep the booze?"

"You must have had a real session with her. There is a bottle under that second bookcase." While I found the bottle, she kept talking. "I finally heard from young Forrester. He was in Washington. I don't know what the hell he was doing in Washington, when he should have been in Boston studying. Funny, he cried when I told him. You wouldn't think he'd cry because Father died."

"It was his father, too, Red. You didn't have a monopoly." I found the bottle, took a swig, and held it out to Rourke, who shook her head. "Mary was crying too."

"Mary cries whenever she wants to. She has a convenient faucet. Tears on or off, hot or cold. But young Forrester is different. He was never around very much. He was frightened of him, timid of him. He's been away at one school or another ever since his mother died. It's funny that he would cry."

"When will he be in?"

"Some time tonight. Now if I could only get my hands on Russell."

I tried the straightforward approach. "Did you find it yet?"

"Find what?"

"The will."

"How did you know it was missing?"

I laughed. "You were right about me, Red. I don't think big and I don't act big. I don't even understand people who think big. Like you—I don't dig you at all. But I have to admit I'm fascinated. You've got me hooked. No matter what, I have to stick around to watch this colossal plot unwind. I got to see what happens in the end."

"You can start off by minding your own business. Right now your business is to find Russ. You have a retainer to make it worth your while to start moving."

"Atta girl, Red. Slap me back into place. Okay. Off I go into the wild blue nowhere looking for your alcoholic oversexed brother."

"Take it easy on me, Maguire. I rip off words pretty fast. I've got a million things on my mind. Try to understand."

"I wonder what would happen if I did understand you, Red. I wonder if I'd fall in love with you or kick you in the ass."

"Right now I'm not in the mood for either," she said. "Go look for Russ and watch out for him. Don't let him charm you the way he does everyone else. Even men whose wives have run off with Russ like him. He's the golden boy."

"You know what I was supposed to do tonight? I was going up to Tina's place for Hungarian goulash and to watch television. Tina's the girl on your gestapo report about me. This job beats the hell out of television. It might even be interesting enough to compensate for missing Tina's goulash."

"You mean she cooks, too?"

"You're jealous, Red." I kissed her and took off.

CHAPTER THREE

FOUND Russell Donnelly two and a half hours after I set out to look for him. It cost thirty dollars in handouts, three calls to New York hotels, a call to a sanitarium for alcoholism in Kansas, a drinking bout with a fag truck driver who knew Donnelly pretty well, climbing up and down a lot of stairs, and finally it cost me a lump in my throat from listening to the sob story of a dice girl who was in love with him.

She had the pasty look of a girl who worked all night and slept all day. She sat behind the green felt table and the arc light on the dice board cast strange shadows on her face. "Hooligan or twenty-six?" she asked.

I took the dice cup, rattled it. "Neither. I want Russ Donnelly."

She ran her tongue over her teeth, blocking any expression from her face. "I don't know any guy named Russ Donnelly. Now beat it."

"A truck driver named Wally White says you know Russ Donnelly."

"I don't know any truck driver named Wally White even. Go on. Beat it."

"This Donnelly guy is tall and has red hair."

"There are lots of guys tall and with red hair. I don't know him personally."

I took ten dollars and laid it on the green felt. "Hooligan," she asked, "or twenty-six?"

"Russell Donnelly."

She shoved the money back. "Take your dough and blow, buddy, or I'll call Al the bartender and have him bounce you out of here."

I looked over at the bar, sized up Al. "Al and who else is going to throw me out of here?"

"Look, don't bother me, will you? I got enough troubles without crackpots. Take your dough and blow like a good boy, huh?"

"Twenty-six," I said. "Two bits on number three." I picked up the dice cup, rattled it and spilled the dice on the green felt. There were three. I threw the dice again. Two threes.

She scribbled the score. "You a cop?"

"Do I look like a cop?"

"Cops are looking better these days."

"Thanks." I shook again. Blank. I was one down.

"What do you want with this guy Donnelly?"

"I don't want him. His sister wants him." I watched the girl's face but it was dead-pan, betraying nothing. I threw the dice again, shook four threes and felt like another drink. "You thirsty?" She shook her head. "Hey, Al," I called behind me. "Set me up with a double Bushmills and soda, will you?"

The girl smiled for the first time. Her teeth needed care. "My old man used to drink Bushmills. He wasn't an Irisher either. He said it took a Polack to appreciate Irish whisky. Go ahead, shake the dice. You're winning."

I threw the dice again, got only one, reached over to the bar, picked up my drink, and left a buck on the counter. "Do you know if Donnelly is in town?"

"I said I didn't know him."

"Wally White said you knew him for sure."

"Who—him or Donnelly?"

"Both of them."

She motioned for me to throw again. "Never heard of Wally White."

"Look. I have no time to play games. I'm looking for Russell Donnelly. He's got a kid sister and she's in trouble and she needs him bad."

"How do I know you're on the level?" She gathered the dice into the cup, handed it to me. "The boss gets mad if customers hang around talking without playing. Keep throwing the dice."

"How do you ever know anybody's on the level?"

She shrugged her shoulders and wrote down the score. "You're one up. Do you see the way sixes are coming up? It was like that last night too. Sixes kept coming up all the time. Anybody who had played sixes all night would have owned the joint today."

"Come on, I haven't got much time."

"If his sister is in trouble, why didn't she come for him? Why'd she send you?"

I swallowed the rest of the drink. "She's been hurt," I said. "She asked me to find her brother."

"Mary has been hurt? How? When? What happened?"

I had her now. She was broken down and the sadness was alive in her eyes again, sadness and compassion and compassion for her sadness. "A car," I said. "There may not be much time. How can I find him?"

"I don't know. I don't know if you're on the level. You could be a process server or something. You could be a hatchet man or something. I don't know. I can't take a chance. He's been so damn sick."

"If anything happens to Mary and you're responsible for keeping him away from her, Donnelly will never forgive you."

"He's been sick. The poor guy has been sick, I really mean sick. He just got out of one of them places where he took the cure. He was so thin and run down. You know what they do to you in places like that. They turn you inside out, wring you dry. He was like a piece of paper and he came down with a cold and he damn near got pneumonia and there was no one to take care of him. He was just sitting there on the bar stool and he fell over like he was dead. I swear it. We brought him to with a shot of booze and wanted to take him to the hospital but the dumb bunny wouldn't go. He just wanted to go and roam the streets some more. He said he didn't have any friends and no family. He didn't have any money. There was no place he could go so I brought him up to my place and took care of him. Don't get me wrong. There's nothing between him and me. Being in the same room with him isn't even right. It's like me and the King of England playing hanky-panky under the table. We're that far apart. I don't care what people say about him, I don't care what he does. He's got class. He reeks of it. It comes out all over him. Class. But he didn't have no classy friends to turn to when he needed them. All there was was a dumb Polack like me."

"So you picked him up off the floor, took him home and fell in love with him."

"Sure. That's the story. It's always the story, isn't it? I got as much right loving him as I do the man in the moon."

"Where is he now, still at your apartment?"

She nodded. "You want to know something funny? He treats me like I was a debutante or Mrs. Astor or somebody. Sick as he was, he was a perfect gentleman. I've never known a man like that. Never in a million years."

"What's your address?"

"You can't let anything happen to him, see. I saved the guy from pneumonia. He might have died or something. I'm not asking for any thanks or anything, I did it because I wanted to. But I don't want him to get sick again. I want somebody to keep taking care of him. He loves his sister Mary. He talks about her all the time. It might kill him if anything happened to her. He might start drinking again. He hasn't touched a drop since he's been at my place. Three weeks and he hasn't touched a drop. Never even asked for it. He could stay cured now. You can't let anything happen to him. You got to promise me that. Go on, promise me."

"Where do you live?"

She was frantic now that she was going to lose him. "You got to promise me. Go on, promise me."

"All right, I promise. Now where do you live?"

She fumbled in her purse, pulled out a key. "He won't answer the doorbell or the phone. So use this, walk right in. Apartment three-thirteen. The address is One-twelve Walton. It's a walk-up. Three flights. Make him take it easy coming down the stairs."

"You must have run into some expenses taking care of him." I pushed two twenties at her. "Maybe this will help."

"Keep your money, mister. I managed all right. I had him for three weeks. That damn movie star didn't even have him that long. I can always have that memory."

"Take the money, kid. Don't be a fool. The family is loaded; they'll never miss it."

She shook her head, pushed it away again. "A lousy forty bucks isn't going to ruin the best thing that ever happened to me."

I held her hand. "Okay. Thanks. You did the right thing."

"Listen," she said, "about that key. Tell Russ he can keep it. I mean, I have another one. Tell him I don't expect him to ever use it but if he gets in trouble again or ... Just tell him to keep the key, huh?"

"I'll tell him."

Russell Donnelly did not awaken when I walked into the apartment. He lay asleep on an in-a-door bed, naked and uncovered. The resemblance to Rourke was amazing—the same color hair, the same textured skin, they were even built alike, lean and tight-muscled. This guy had class built in. Even without clothes and in the cheap bed in the cheap apartment, he looked rich, well-bred and well-educated. Rourke was right about what could happen to this guy in the movies. If the female public saw what I was looking at, there would be more than panic in the streets. There would be a lot of complaints in a lot of bedrooms.

The radio next to the bed was blaring out the last inning of a double-header. I turned it off. On top of the radio were three medicine bottles, a glass of water and a spoon. The room itself was in perfect order, sentiment-inscribed pillows from Army and Navy bases carefully arranged on a sofa, amusement park figurines and prizes lined up neatly on the dresser, freshly laundered curtains tied back on clean windows overlooking a dirty alley.

I touched his shoulder, shook him gently. "Hey, Donnelly, wake up."

He stirred, opened his eyes, saw me, stretched his arms over his head and grabbed the iron headboard. "Hi. You a friend of Wanda's?"

"No. I came looking for you."

"You got a cigarette?" I handed him a pack. "Light it for me, will you. My hand is still shaky." He rolled over, flicked on the radio. "How did the second game come out?"

"I don't know. I didn't listen." I handed him the lighted cigarette. "You'd better get some clothes on."

"What for?"

"You're coming with me."

His face seemed to register no emotion. He wasn't surprised, frightened, bewildered. "Where are we going?"

"Home," I answered.

"Your house?"

I shook my head. "No, your house."

He was silent, listening to the final score, and then turned off the radio. "As far as I know, this is the only home I have."

"Look, my name is John Maguire. I'm a friend of your sister's."

Now he sat up. "Mary. Is Mary all right?"

"Mary is just fine. But I'm a friend of Rourke's. She sent me to find you."

"Rourke sent you to find me. How did you do it?"

"Mary gave me the lead; I took it from there."

"You a detective, private eye?"

My Irish went up. Just like he looked like class, I looked like a cop or detective. "I'm a lawyer, but I'm not working. Like I said, I'm a friend of Rourke's. I'm doing her a favor." I sat on the bed. "Listen, there's no point beating around this. Your father died last night or this morning. Rourke wants you. She thinks you should be there."

Donnelly took a hard swallow of the cigarette. His hand did shake pretty bad. He said, "How is Rourke; how is she taking it?"

"Like a soldier. What did you expect?"

"I don't know. I never thought about it. I never thought of what she would be like without him. Poor Rourke. It'll be hard for her." He pulled his legs up, rested his chin on his knees. "I've seen Mary and young Forrester as much as I could, but I haven't seen Rourke in years. How is she, Maguire?"

"She's fine, I guess. I don't see much of her."

Now he gave me the once over. "Where do you fit in? Are you in love with her?"

"No."

"Oh, it's that way." He seemed to know more than I told him. "Tell me something, Maguire, how is she in bed? It's something I've always wondered about. She's either hot as hell or cold as hell."

"You'd better get dressed."

He smiled, a good healthy, honest grin. "I forgot there are gentlemen left in the world. Sorry."

"It's all right. It's a funny question for a guy to ask about his own sister."

"I'm a funny guy and she's a funny sister. You don't want to tell me, huh?"

"How do you know I even sleep with her?"

"It figures," he answered. "She was a virgin for a long time. I don't know what she was saving it for. It used to drive guys nuts. It would have had to be a guy like you."

"How do you know what kind of a guy I am?"

"I can tell by looking. You got an honest Irish mug, you're straight from the shoulder and you don't take any shit from anyone." He squashed out the cigarette. "How's my character analysis?"

"Pretty good."

He smiled again. It's hard to explain the effect of his smile. It's the way a kid smiles—uncomplicated, uncontrived, completely outgoing. This man was supposed to be one of the most dissolute guys around. Rumors accused him of everything—being a dope addict, a gigolo, a sex maniac, a fairy and a drunk. And yet he smiled like that, clean and happy. "You still don't want to tell me how she is in bed?"

"Why is it so important?"

This time he laughed. "Hey, you sound like you're in training to be a psychiatrist. That's a very psychoanalytical-type question, why is it so important. I'll give you a very unpsychiatric answer. I am a man who likes sex. Some guys like golf, some collect stamps. I like sex. I like it best of all when I do it. Next to that I like hearing about other people."

"Something just hit me. I told you your father is dead and you have no reaction."

"You're wrong, Maguire. I am reacting. If you were a hot psychoanalyst you'd know that."

"I'm a mug with a law degree. In my world when you tell a guy his father is dead, he cries or he laughs or he gets drunk or he goes to church. But you want to know what kind of a lay your sister is."

"Fascinating, isn't it? People are fascinating—what they do, how they react. I like people real well. Do you?"

"Listen, I think we ought to get on the ball. Rourke has some kind of a big deal going on. I don't know what it is but you figure in it. The sooner I show up with you, the better." I considered for a minute before I went on. "There's something else. I got Mary to tell me how to find you. I made a promise and I guess I've got to keep it. I told her that if I found you, I'd tell you what happened and that Rourke wants you. If you wanted to go home, I'd take you. If you didn't, I promised I'd never tell Rourke I had found you."

"You mean I have a choice. You're not going to strongarm me into going home?"

"I promised Mary."

"Poor Mary," he said. "Of all of us, I feel most sorry for Mary."

"What's your decision?"

Donnelly got out of bed, put on a robe, checked a clock and came around to take some medicine and washed it down with water. "I guess I've been sick as hell. At my best I'm not what is known as a stable guy. I took the cure a few weeks ago, got into a mess with an orderly at the sanitarium who was bringing me stuff in from the outside. They kicked us both out; I guess he took me on a toot for a few days and I caught cold or something. Anyway, I'm pretty shaky. Maybe I need a drink. Hey, why don't you run to a store and get a bottle? We can kill it and I can work up some energy. Good idea?" He looked at me, saw the expression on my face. "You're right. It's a lousy idea. I'd be right back on the bottle again. Okay, let's say it. I'm scared. I'm scared of going home again."

"Your father is dead. He can't hurt you now."

"He can't? A lot you know. You'd make a lousy psychiatrist. You're a nice guy, Maguire. I like the way you talk and I like the way you look but you've got a low-ball sensitivity."

I laughed. "A lot you know. Want me to drag out my crystal ball?"

"Sure. Go ahead."

"You want to know how she is in bed. Could only be one reason. You must have tried when you were a kid."

"Not bad, Maguire. You're showing promise again. Continue."

"Isn't that enough?" For a minute I wondered what the hell I was doing there, talking to him, making with the crystal ball. If I had been on schedule, my shoes would have been off, Tina's goulash in my belly, and the fight raging on television.

"When we were little we came from another city into a big house with strange people. There were only the two of us, me and Rourke. Everyone else was a stranger. Even my father. We had lived in Atlanta with my grandparents until my father showed up one day and took us away. Rourke was the only thing I had to cling to. I always looked up to her. I always… Oh, what the hell, this is all talk for nothing. That was all a long time ago and it's different now."

"Is it?"

That smile again. "The hell it is. It's exactly the same."

"So what do you do? Go or stay?"

"Go," he said. "Mary and young Forrester will need me."

"I'm glad, Russ." And we shook hands because it seemed the perfectly normal thing to do at that moment. "I'll call Rourke and tell her I've found you. Where's the phone?"

"In the dressing room. There ought to be some nickels on top of the box. I'll get dressed."

I dialed the number, finally got through to Rourke. "Where the hell have you been?" she asked.

"I've been looking for your brother. I've found him."

"Good. I can't hold the news back one minute longer. The undertaker has the casket in the hearse waiting for my call. I have all the releases prepared for the newspapers. Everything is set to go. Get him here as fast as you can."

"Okay."

"Maguire?"

"What?"

"Is he sober?"

"Yes, he's very sober. He's been pretty sick, Red. Pneumonia. He's all right now, but weak. I'd take it easy on him; not to rush him into anything."

"Did you ask him about the movies?"

I thought for a minute. "What movies?"

"Did you ask him if he was going to Hollywood?"

"No. There wasn't time. We've been talking about sex."

"Well, you couldn't discuss it with a more well-informed person. Hurry up," she said and hung up.

Donnelly was dressed when I went back in. "You have any money on you, Maguire?"

"Sure. What for?"

"Wanda. The girl who lives here. She's taken care of me, paid for the doctor, the medicine."

"I tried to give her some dough, but she wouldn't take it. She told me not to spoil the only decent thing that ever happened to her." I held out the key she had given me. "She says for you to keep this, use it if you want to or need help."

He shook his head. "Leave it on the table there. I'll never use it and I know what it is giving someone a key for your door and night after night lying awake listening for the sound of it turning in the lock and never hearing anything. I wouldn't do that to her." He started to make the bed. I gave him a hand and we lifted it up into the wall and closed the doors over it. He dumped the medicine in a wastebasket, washed the spoon and glass and put them in a cabinet.

"You'd make a good murderer," I commented.

"You mean no evidence? I guess I would make a good murderer at that. Let's go, Maguire."

"Don't you have any other clothes?"

He pulled a plastic-cased toothbrush from his pocket. "This is it. The rest of my stuff must be in California. I can borrow a razor from my brother. Do you have a black tie you can lend me? I ought to wear a black tie."

"I'll dig one up for you."

"Maguire, where do you figure in all this? I mean, do you deliver me and take off or do you stick around?"

"I stick around to watch the fun."

"Do me a favor, will you? Keep an eye on me, huh?"

He seemed unsteady, teetering. I put my arm around his shoulder. "Sure thing," I said and led him out.

Our taxi had to wait while the hearse backed out of the driveway. A funeral wreath had already been hung on one of the double doors, a long arrangement of white flowers and waxy leaves highlighted by the coach lights flanking the doorway. Darkness had begun, the light night descending.

Russell said, "It's a funny way to be coming home. I cried when my step-mother Dolly died. I was a grown man and I cried like a baby. I should feel something now, shouldn't I?" He rubbed his hands together and I could tell he was thinking of how good a stiff shot would feel, warming his belly. "I don't feel anything inside," he said. "Nothing. Just hollow."

"It'll be okay," I said because I didn't know what else to say.

"I wonder if I will get used to his being dead? Even now, I know he's dead but it's like the other times I've come home, wondering what he'll be mad about this time, what he'll raise hell about. He'll be sitting in the chair in the library with that look on his face." He hesitated. "I wonder if they embalmed him with a smile on his face, a look of serenity." The hearse was past us and we moved up the driveway. "They did that to Dolly when she died, embalmed her with a smile on her face. But she was like that, always smiling. They ought to have fixed him to look stern and solemn. When a man is dead he ought to look as much as possible the way he did when he was alive. When I die they ought to lay me out with my fly open."

I paid off the driver, helped Russ out of the cab. "Feel all right?"

"I'm scared, Maguire. I'm scared to go in. How about ducking up the street for one drink?"

"Sooner or later you have to face it. Better do it now and get it over with." I took his arm firmly. I needed a drink myself.

He stopped outside the side door, looked up at the house. "They ought to cut back the vines. They're all dead. They don't have leaves any more. They look like skeletons clinging to the stone."

"Pull yourself together."

"I'm together. I was wondering about the vines, wondering why they don't cut them back."

I pushed him up to the door and tried it; it was open. Instantly there was the heavy smell of flowers, a different smell from flowers in a vase of flowers in a flower shop or flowers in a field. Only flowers near a coffin smell like this. Straight ahead through the partially opened parlor doors, surrounded by flickering candlelight, was the large, dark bulk of the casket under a blanket of flowers. Donnelly turned away. "Close the doors. Close them. Hurry up, close the doors." He was near panic. I left him huddled in the narrow passage, ran across the reception hall and closed the doors to the room where the body lay.

"It's all right now," I said.

"I'm behaving like a kid, a damn, scared kid."

"Come on."

"Wait a minute." He turned around, relaxed when he saw that the doors were closed, and looked around him. "All my life I've been coming in through this door, the family entrance. You see those seats? Under them we used to keep all our junk—boots, baseball bats, tennis rackets. Say, I'll bet the stuff is still there. They never clean anything out of this morgue." He went down on his knees, raised the lid of the seat and came up with a tennis racket. He tested it. The guts were weak and limp. "I told you they never throw anything away. I bet this has been here for fifteen years. I used to have a pretty good backhand." He swung the racket and it hit against the oak paneling. He had the racket in a firm grip. "It's all right now, let's go in."

On the marble floor he hopped from black square to another, not touching the white squares—a children's game. The center of the hall had a large rectangle of metal on the floor with some design and inscription now worn down. This was a safety zone, because he stood here with both feet on the ground, swinging the tennis racket. He whistled loudly, a special whistle, a signal.

After a minute Mary's voice came from upstairs. "Russ? Russ, is it you?"

"Come on, Mary. Come on."

She flew down the stairs into his arms, crying, laughing and talking all at once. "I'm glad you're home, Russ. I'm glad you're home."

"A very touching sight." It was Rourke at the doorway to the library. She had changed into a plain black dress, and her hair was tied back away from her face. Her voice and appearance had the sudden effect of a quick freeze. Mary stopped jabbering instantly. Russ froze, the tennis racket outstretched. It even got to me. I think I was standing there with my jaw dropped and my feet duck-style.

I would have said something but I didn't know what to say. We all just stood there in the silence. Finally, Russ broke the ice with a smile. "Hello, Red," he said. "Long time no see." He walked toward her, leaned down to kiss her, and she turned her cheek. "You look good, Red." He touched her hair. "I had forgotten you were so damn beautiful."

She smoothed her hair where he had touched it. "You look awful, Russ. You're so thin and pale."

"I'm glad to see you, Red, I really am."

"Damn it, I'm glad to see you, too."

"Hey, those aren't tears, are they? I don't look as bad as all that."

Awkwardly, tentatively, she put her hand on his face. "Just at the end when he was so very sick, so very thin, he looked like you or you looked like him." She smiled. "It's been so damn quiet around here without you, Russ."

Mary came to life, ran over to them. "Isn't it wonderful! When Sonny gets here we'll all be together just like we used to be. Won't it be wonderful?"

"Look," I said, knowing an exit cue when I heard one, "I'd better take off. There's a pot of goulash growing cold."

"Stick around, Maguire," Rourke said. "You're not through yet."

"I got news for you, Red," I said, "I come and go as I please. Remember that."

Russ came up to me. "Hey, John boy. Stick around, huh?" He winked at me. "Why don't we all have a drink. We could all do with a drink."

"Suits me." I needed one.

We sat in the dark, depressing library. The children made small talk while I made a perfunctory survey of the books. The butler brought in a tray with a couple of bottles, a bucket of ice and glasses. Russ took over the bartending job and handled it neatly considering that he never let go of the tennis racket. Mary didn't drink. Rourke had a highball and I had a double shot straight and then another shot which I sipped slowly. Russ poured himself a drink, had it right to his mouth, then put it down without touching it.

Rourke was explaining the funeral arrangements, talking about governors and ambassadors and senators, giving a run-down on the activities for the next few days. I excused myself and went to the john, then found a phone and called Tina. "Don't get mad," I started out; "I'm working."

"On who, or should I say whom?"

"This is legit. A nice big, fat fee. Enough so maybe we can bounce off for a week in Florida."

"I've heard this before."

"But this time it's going to happen. You can even go out and buy a new bathing suit."

"Maybe I can convert a perfectly good pot of goulash into something fetching for the beach."

"Look, Tina, don't get sore. You know me. I'm not dependable but eventually I show."

"Sure. Last time it was two weeks and you showed up sunburned with long claw marks on your back."

"I'll call you when the job is over. Keep an eye on my office for me."

"I'm a sap," she said. "I love you."

"That's a good girl. How was the goulash?"

"I never tasted it. I lost my appetite."

"Well, work it up. I'll be around eventually."

They were still at it in the library, Rourke talking and the others listening.

Mary said, "What about the will? Did you find the will?"

"We'll talk about it later."

"I'd better get off my feet for a while," Russ said. "I guess I was sicker than I knew. I'm weak."

"Come on, Russ," Mary said, taking his hand. "I'll fix up your room for you and you can take a nap until Sonny gets here. I'll have cook fix you some soup. Remember Mother always used to fix us soup when we were sick. I'll tell cook exactly how to make it."

Russ said, "You'll be around, won't you, Maguire?" I nodded. He started out the room, happened to look up over the fireplace, and stopped. "How come the light is out over Dolly's portrait?" He went over, flicked the switch, peeked behind to see if the fixture was plugged in. "For Christ's sake, doesn't anyone know how to run a household around here? How could you let the light go out over the portrait?" He pulled the long cord of the servant's bell. The portrait over the fireplace was of a young girl, beautiful in a pale, delicate way. "You did it purposely, didn't you, Red? You knew it was the one thing Grandpa Forrester always insisted on. The light was never to go off over the portrait."

"You're getting in an uproar over nothing," Rourke said. "We never use this room. What's the difference?"

"There's a lot of difference. This is Dolly's house, and don't you forget it." The butler was at the door. "Why isn't that light on over the portrait?" The butler was startled, looked at Rourke for direction. She shrugged her shoulders in disgust. "Well, answer me."

"I don't know, sir."

"Well, get a light in and make sure it works and do it now."

The servant waited, looked at Rourke again. She nodded her approval. For a minute I thought Russ was going to take his untouched drink off the tray, but Mary took his hand and together they went upstairs.

"He's such a damn sentimental slob about Dolly Forrester," Rourke said. "He was always the apple of her eye. She even preferred him to her own children. She spoiled him rotten. I blame her for the way Russ is."

"He's a good guy."

"Has he charmed you already, Maguire? I thought you were harder to get to." She sat down in the chair by the fireplace, obviously her father's chair. "Shut the door, get yourself another drink and sit down."

I took my time following instructions, finally lay down on the couch. "Okay, Red, what's the pitch."

"I found the will. I found Father's will."

"Good for you."

"I'm counting on you for loyalty, Maguire. Loyalty to me personally. Not loyalty to the family necessarily, but loyalty to me. Is that clear?"

"How many times do I have to tell you about me? I don't promise anything. Give me the pitch and I'll do what I think is right."

She stood up, paced the room. "First let me give you some background. The Forrester Industries are made up of seven units. The president of each unit sits on the board of control. My father, of course, was chairman of the board. What he said was law. For the last five years I've been my father's right hand. I've learned the Forrester Industries cold, I know what makes them work, how they work and how they can work better. I know each subsidiary as well as any man in the organization. I've walked timberlands, I've gone down in mines, I've worked in steel mills, everything. I know it all cold. I have it all here right in my hand."

"You don't have to convince me. I believe you." Funny how I felt about her just then. I was awed by her. Disregarding sex, this was a person you had to respect, a person who was smart and keen, shrewd and informed. This was a big-league operator, a bigger league than I had ever played in or come close to playing in. Regarding sex, I wanted her pretty bad.

"Eight months ago, my father began to be sick. It was cancer. We knew it right away, both of us. We made a decision to keep his sickness secret. I took over direct control in his name. I put through a lot of plans and expansion programs that my father was not in favor of. But I knew what I was doing. Except for one mining thing, everything worked big. We've bought three newspapers in the Northwest. That's a big new area for expansion. Watch it. Spokane is sitting right under the biggest mining bonanza in Canada. It's unbelievable what's going to happen in the Northwest. We have three department store shopping centers going in outlying suburban areas. We're late, but not too late. We have the money and the staying power. We can outprice the stores that beat us to the punch. I've done all this, Maguire, do you understand? I've done all this by myself. I've plotted it, planned it and put it into action."

"Bully," I said.

"I don't mean to sound conceited," she said. She came over, sat on the floor near me, put her hand on my leg. "Look, you know I can be human, I can be a woman. But you can't conceive the thrill of controlling what I've controlled, of taking desperate flings for millions of dollars and being right."

"It's over my head, but go on; finish the story."

"My father had enemies. Lots of them. Business enemies. The family owns the controlling stock in the Forrester Industries. Father owned it all in his name. Each of the children have a little bit but not enough to mean anything. There's one man in particular who was out to get Father's scalp. A man named Dexter Cummings. Ever hear of him?"

"Vaguely. A manipulator of some kind, isn't he?"

"A manipulator of the very best kind and, incidentally, a brother-in-law of one Mathew Lawrence, president of Forrester Steel. Each of the presidents owns stock in the Industries. We didn't want to relinquish it but they forced us into it over the years. They got stock bonus and gradually they've accumulated a lot. Dexter Cummings has been buying as much stock on the open market as he could get for the last seven years. He's bought it under his own name, Mathew's name, dummy corporations, assorted relatives and God knows who. None of the presidents of the subsidiaries were loyal to Father. Given a chance they'll throw in with Cummings in a minute. Altogether they represent a damn big block of stock."

I sat up. "Enough to kick out the Forrester-Donnelly interests?"

"When the word gets out that my Father is dead, the stock will drop. Little investors all over the country who had faith in my father, faith in the Industries, will get scared when they know he is no longer at the helm. They'll sell. Cummings will buy up fast. I have my brokers working on it now, but Cummings will get his share and maybe more."

"I don't get it. You still have controlling interest, don't you? I mean even if Cummings controls every outstanding share you still have more than he does."

She lighted a cigarette, blew out the match, threw it on the floor. "My father had the control. That's why the will was so important. If he left it all to me there would be no problem. I would simply take over. They'd fuss and fume and there would be a riot here and there but in the end they couldn't stop me. I would have control and that would be that. The presidents might quit, pull out when a woman took over as chairman. But that wouldn't matter. There's enough money to buy up their stock and I've been training my own people in each one of the subsidiaries. I can pull up a new executive team without too much trouble."

"But he didn't leave it all to you."

"I don't understand it," she said. "I don't know why. He had no use for any of the others. They were no good. I was everything to him, Maguire. For these last eight months I was his breath and his strength. I'm not complaining. I loved him and I would have done everything for him anyway. But I don't understand why he did what he did. He loved me. He knew I could handle everything. There must have been a reason why he did what he did. If I only knew what I did to make him distrust me."

"What did he do exactly? Do you know what the will says?"

Rourke stood up, walked over to the empty fireplace. "The will states that all the money, all the stocks and bonds, all the interests in the Forrester Industries is left jointly to the four children. Even Russ. He even included Russ. The whole estate is left to the four children jointly and we are to decide who gets control, who is to run the Industries. Don't you see what this means?"

It was very clear. If one of the children took his share and beat it over to the opposition, Dexter Cummings would gain control of the Industries and Rourke would be out on her ear. It was that simple. "What are you going to do, Red?"

"Convince them that we have to stick together, and that I am the person to hold control. I don't care about the money, Maguire. The money doesn't mean anything There's plenty. We'll all be loaded. But I want to keep on running the Industries, expand them, develop them. I can do a big job. Cummings would ruin us financially. His records with other companies is appalling. He coddles labor. He pretends to be a great humanitarian. He'd try to turn the Forrester Industries into a charitable foundation before he was through."

"Who do you think will give you trouble—Russ, Mary or young Forrester?"

"I don't know. They all hate me, you know that. They're afraid of me. I know I haven't been a hundred per cent right with them. I've had no patience, I've had no time to be understanding. They don't have what it takes, Maguire, and there wasn't time for me to pay attention to anyone without brainpower. Russ has the brainpower but he's drunk and screwed himself useless. Sonny is a dope. He has no imagination, no vision. It's not all my fault. We've been such a damn mixed-up family. There was no room for love; everybody was always playing everyone against the other."

"It's too late now to be nice to them," I said.

"I can't change toward them, Maguire. In my own way I'm as honest as you are. Not even for this could I lie and cheat and pretend that I love them and think that underneath it all they're great." She nibbled at her thumbnail, clicking it against her teeth. "What do you think, Maguire?"

"I don't know. There's a lot to think about. Me, for example. What am I doing in this mess?" She didn't answer. "You know what you are to me, Red? Up until today you were nothing but an occasional roll in the hay. That's all I knew about you. It was enough, until today."

"And today?"

"Today you're all of a sudden a tycoon and you're using me for something I can't figure. What am I here for? Bird dog? Stud dog? Not as a lawyer, certainly. If there are ten thousand lawyers in the United States, nine thousand nine hundred and ninety-nine would be better equipped for this than I. I collect a good bill. I get accidents settled fast and I'm a whiz with labor union problems. But not this. This requires a chief justice. So why am I here? Tell me that, Red. Why am I here?"

Softly, she said, "To help me."

"Why? Because I love you or you love me?"

"Isn't it enough that I need you?"

I shook my head. "No. When you came to my apartment in the middle of the night and needed me, it was enough then. Nobody could get hurt but you or me. Now there are lots of people involved. It's not enough."

"What do you want me to say? What can I say to you that will make you help me?"

"How *can* I help you? What can I do? I found your brother, I held your sister's head while she threw up. I can answer telephone calls and put the light bulb in over the portrait if the butler ever brings it. What else can I do?"

"Look, Maguire." She turned away. "No, don't look. I don't think I can say it if I look at you." I waited. "You mean something to me," she said. "You represent something. I may be only an occasional roll in the hay to you but it's not that way with me. I'm not saying I'm in love with you. I'm saying that with you, I'm a woman. When I'm with you, I'm different from the way I usually am. I'm not fighting, I'm not scratching, I'm not commanding. I can't be that way here. My whole life has been me against the others. I've had to be tough, I've had to be smart. When I was an adolescent, I used to watch Dolly with the other children, with Russ and her own children. They used to be in the playroom upstairs, having tea parties, playing masquerades, singing and dancing. When one of them fell or got hurt, they would run to Dolly, put their head in her lap and she would soothe them. I could never become a part of that. My heart used to ache to join in, to be hurt and to be comforted by Dolly. But I didn't belong, I was from the outside. Russ didn't belong either, and I hated him for being part of it. Dolly never liked me. I was my father's daughter, part of his life before he came here. She tried to be nice to me, I know that. It was no good. I never belonged. I belonged only to my father."

"I still don't get it," I said.

"I'm trying to say that until today you knew me as a woman, not as who I am, what I am here with the others. Maybe you can make them see that part of me. Maybe with you here to slap me down, I can be more human. I know my faults, Maguire. I know them too damn well. I have no friends. I have no lovers. I have only you."

"I'm a stranger to you, Red."

"Not really. You can't live with a man and not know what he's made of. People trust you. God knows I don't trust anyone, but I trust you; not to do what I want you to do—I trust you to do the decent thing, what you think is right. They will trust you, too. I think Mary and Russ do already. Russ was leaning on you. Mary carried on about you after you left. She thinks you're divine."

"And you?"

"I think you're divine, too."

"Turn around and come here," I said.

It was wonderful to kiss her again with no bars between us, no defenses to block the flow of what we were feeling for each other. "You know what I wish, Red? I wish Dexter Cummings would run off with the whole damn show. Then you and I would go to Mexico maybe. Rent a sailboat and fish and make love. Once a week we'd get dressed up and go into Mexico City and all the guys would say, how did an Irish mug like that snag such a woman. They'd be jealous as hell."

"I wish I could wish that too. I wish I didn't want this other thing, this power I want, these plans I have. I wish I'd be content to be in that sailboat and fish and make love. I'm not made that way."

I rubbed my nose in her hair and maybe loved her then. "I know you're not, Red. I'm sorry for you."

"What about it, Maguire? Will you help me?"

"I'll stick around and see what I can do. I'm not promising anything. It depends. Maybe you're wrong and the others are right. If that's the way it turns out, that's the way it will be."

The discreet coughing by the butler broke us up. "I have the light bulb," he said, "and Mr. Forrester has arrived. There is a young lady with him. In what room shall I put her?"

"A young lady! That's great. Just what we need. I wonder what library he found her in. What does she look like, Brooks? How thick are her glasses?" Rourke had tightened up, the defenses were back in order.

"She's very attractive, Miss Rourke." He smiled a little. "She is not the kind of young lady you would have expected Mr. Forrester to bring home. No offense, of course."

"Well, this sounds very interesting. What would you guess, Brooks? A bubble dancer? A bareback rider in a circus?"

"She seems quite nice, Miss Rourke. What room shall I give her?"

"Let me see. We have Mr. Maguire in the Dutch Room, haven't we?"

"Hey, wait a minute," I said. "What's with me and the Dutch Room? I got a home. I'm not living here."

"For the duration of the emergency you are," she said. "I didn't specify this as a nine-to-five job, did I? Give Brooks the key to your apartment and he'll bring some of your stuff over."

"Not so fast, Red. I'm not sure I ..."

"Come on, Maguire. A deal is a deal."

I shrugged my shoulders, took my house key and handed it to the butler. "Brooks, if there happens to be an attractive young lady in my apartment, tell her to make herself at home and I'll show up eventually."

"Put the young lady in the Chinese Room," Rourke said.

"It sounds like I'd like the Chinese Room better."

Rourke shook her head. "You'll be crazy about the Dutch Room. It's full of blue and white tiles and old wooden shoes with dead plants in them." Then, to Brooks, "Tell Mr. Forrester to come in here."

"He's in the parlor, Miss Rourke, with your father. The young lady is waiting in the hall. The newspapers have come out with the story of Mr. Donnelly's passing. It has been on the radio and cook said that the television has been showing some old newsreel clippings of your father. The telephone hasn't stopped ringing. We have told everyone that you are receiving callers after nine."

"Thank you, Brooks."

"What about the young lady?"

"Take her bags up to the Chinese Room. I'll figure out what to do with her." When he had gone she peeked out into the hall. "What do you know, she isn't half bad. Such a dumb thing to do, bring a woman here at a time like this. The worst possible time. Do you see what I'm up against? Do you see why it's so hard for me? For twenty-five years he never looked at a woman. I don't think he knew what they were for. All of a sudden he's bringing them home."

"Want me to take over, Red?" I straightened my tie.

"If she's going to be embarrassing, get her the hell out of here. Put her up in a hotel or something. You handle it."

This time I took a look through the door, let out a whistle. "Say, maybe we could both use the Dutch Room."

"Get out of here, Maguire. Go to work."

I didn't know what to say to the stranger in the hall so I said, "I could stand a drink, how about you?"

She cased me carefully, understood that in my own way I was a stranger there too. "Who are you?"

"My name's John Maguire. What's yours?"

"Straight gin. Where do we find it?"

This was the kind of woman I understood, my kind, from the same side of the tracks. She was handsome, handsomely put together, not as young as she looked at first glance, still under forty but pushing it hard. She was tall, very lean. Wonderful eyes, black and deep. Her black hair was pulled slick away from her face and two gray streaks were applied from the center part. She wore a black skirt and a long-sleeved, high-neck black sweater ornamented only by a huge, hand-forged abstract copper pendant which hung from a chain and landed in exactly the right position between her breasts. She was wearing very unbecoming flat-heeled shoes and I figured young Forrester Donnelly didn't quite make it to reach her.

I took her hand. "We can try the kitchen. There's a butler named Brooks. He'll know." We wandered through a succession of doors and halls until we found the kitchen. Brooks set up a couple of bottles in the narrow pantry. "How do you take your gin?"

"Like a man," she said. "Straight."

I poured. "Say when." After a minute, she said it and I poured myself another drink, sipped it and studied her. This was a slicked-up version of the intense young woman who had haunted American campuses in the thirties. She was the girl who carried picket signs, thought Trotsky was dandy, loved Mozart and jazz with equal passion, fought against reaction on every level. This was the same girl grown into a woman, refined by age and changed by the changing times. Her nose had been remodeled by skilled surgical hands into a ski-slide shape and her eyes were carefully made up with black to compensate for the radical fervor which had once burned in them. All in all she was a well-turned-out package, something I could understand and handle. I didn't see how Forrester Donnelly had a chance with her.

"Do you have me catalogued yet, Mr. Maguire?"

I nodded. "I know all about you but I don't know your name."

"My name is Sylvia Newman."

"It's your move," I said.

Her fingernails were long enough to be claws. "I don't know where you fit," she said. "Forrester hasn't mentioned you. I know all about the others but I don't know about you."

"I'm the old family friend, the legal retainer."

"You don't look the type."

"I'm not. I've only been an old family friend and retainer for a few hours. It will take some getting used to. That's my status in relation to the Donnelly family. What's yours?"

"A little more gin," she said. "I'm here because Forrester would not come here without me. He wants to marry me."

"Not bad. You could do worse. Why don't you let him talk you into it."

"Don't be impertinent, Mr. Maguire. Forrester is in love with me."

"And you with him?"

"I'm very fond of him. Don't underestimate him or his potentialities."

"I don't underestimate anyone with that much dough." I poured another drink. "What did you used to do for a living?"

"I work for the State Department. I am a minor authority on Rumania."

"Rumania, huh? I wondered what the hell ever happened to Rumania. How did you get to be a minor authority on Rumania?"

"You know how Washington is," she said, "particularly the State Department. I was a researcher on the Middle East. The competition was too rough. There are so many authorities on the Middle East. I shopped for a neglected country, found Rumania, boned up, presented myself as an authority, and in the last few years I think I've really become a genuine authority. I'm planning to write a book after Forrester and I are married."

"Then you have let him talk you into it, getting married, I mean."

"Look, Mr. Maguire, let's understand each other right now. I know what to expect here; Forrester has warned me and I didn't need any warning. Everyone will think I'm marrying Donnelly money. I can't help what they think. I am going to marry Forrester Donnelly for reasons known to him and to me. It is our business and no one else is concerned. We're both adults."

"Yeah," I said, "particularly you." I grabbed her hand inches away from my face. "You've got spirit, Sylvia, but save it for the Donnellys. Don't try using it on an Irish mug. They hit back."

"I'm going to find Forrester."

"Not yet. They're having a family reunion. Strangers keep out. You and me are strangers." I filled her glass again. "Don't get me wrong. I don't care if you marry the kid or not. It's your business and his. You're going to have a hell of a fight with Rourke. I'm not even sure Mary and Russ are going to take you to their hearts right off. But I don't matter."

"None of you matter," she said.

"How come you got together with a guy like Forrester? How did you meet him?"

"He came to Washington to do some research with a professor who escaped from Rumania, a delightful old man who is an expert on the Crusades. I met Forrester at his house."

"And it was love at first sight."

"On the contrary. I thought he was a dull young man. It was only after talking to him for a long time that I came to have an inkling of the depth of his mind, the potential of his brain power. All his intelligence has been so misdirected. Studying the Middle Ages is no outlet for his mind."

"I don't know the kid," I explained. "I only have the family report on him."

"His family doesn't know him either. Not yet. It took me time. I didn't know who he was at first. I didn't realize his connection with the Forrester Industries. When I did, many things made sense. His fascination with the Middle Ages, serfdom, slaves and masters. How like his father! The feudal holdings—how like the Forrester Industries! What he was doing was sublimating all his hatred in the Dark Ages, hiding out doing research of injustices even greater than those he had grown up with. Forrester and I have talked about this a great deal with a psychiatrist friend of mine in Washington. It's been fascinating. It's helped Forrester so much to understand himself, to see why he chose the Middle Ages of all the things in the world to become an expert on. And understanding this has freed him to go beyond feudal history, to have courage to face today."

"This whole thing is getting out of my range."

"I don't think so, Mr. Maguire. I think you follow me step by step. I think in your initial catalogue of me, you catalogued me just right."

"Let me tell you something. First with me comes the body. Then comes the soul. The intellect makes out a poor third."

"My body gets me around," she said, "my soul is inactive but available and my intellect goes as fast as hell."

"You're in third, I'm still in first. Would you like to shift into my gear?"

"The body?" She shook her head. "I'm too mature to get side-tracked in the bushes."

"You just haven't been in the right bushes with the right guy."

"And just where are your bushes, Mr. Maguire?"

"I'm sleeping in the Dutch Room," I said. "Knock on my windmill any time." I took her arm. "Shall we join the ladies?"

All hell was breaking loose in the front of the house. The doors to the parlor were open and young Forrester was helping Mary out of the room. A maid with a scrub bucket was on her knees on the carpet. Russell was standing at the coffin, immobile, his attention so fixed on the corpse that he was unaware of anything going on about him. Rourke was in the middle of it all, shouting at the maid, calling to Russ and shrieking at Mary.

"But Rourke," Mary was saying. "You shouldn't have forced me. I knew I would do it. The smell of the flowers was so strong. I told you I didn't want to." Mary saw me. "I told you this afternoon I didn't want to see him dead. I threw up on the rug again." She broke away from her brother, ran to me. "Why weren't you here? You promised you would help."

I patted her head, held her to me. "What's the difference, Mary. It's a lousy-looking rug anyway."

She relaxed a little and giggled. "Yes, I suppose it is."

Forrester and Sylvia Newman were huddled in conversation. He was two inches shorter than she, not a bad-looking guy. He wore heavy glasses and had a lingering case of adolescent skin. He was built short and stocky, certainly not from the same strain as Rourke and Russell. I watched as Forrester steered Sylvia toward Rourke. This was a meeting I wanted to see. But Rourke ignored everybody; she walked into the parlor and stood beside Russ. talking a mile a minute to him. He was frozen in position and didn't seem to hear her voice.

"I'm Forrester Donnelly," Forrester said. We shook hands. "Rourke told me you were here to help us and I'm grateful. And thank you for looking after Sylvia for me. I guess she told you that we were engaged. I haven't told Rourke or anyone yet."

"You may be smart to let it ride until the first shock of confusion is over," I said. "I'm glad to know you." I glanced over at Sylvia. "Congratulations. I think you've got yourself quite a girl."

"Thank you." He shook my hand again. "You'll never know how wonderful she really is," he said. "She's made a new man out of me."

Rourke was back in the hall again. "This thing is going to drive me right out of my mind. Why must you all behave like children? Why can't any of you stand up and accept responsibility? Maguire, see what you can do about Russ. He's standing there in a trance. I can't get him to move." She dismissed me with a turn of her head. "Mary, comb your hair and take off that lipstick. It looks frightful. If you're going to defy your father you might at least wait until he's under the ground. Have you no respect? Doesn't it mean anything to you?"

I grabbed her before she got into the library. "Rourke," I said, "you haven't met Miss Newman yet." I led her to Sylvia. "Miss Newman is a friend of Forrester's."

Rourke's female intuition went to work. Her back stiffened and fire flared out of her eyes. She only nodded her head, said nothing.

Sylvia Newman smiled. "I'm sorry," she said, "about your father. I realize this is a terrible time for you. I hope I won't be in the way. Forrester insisted I come home with him."

Young Donnelly lumbered out from the shadows, stood beside Sylvia. "You bet I did," he said, and stood awkwardly waiting for someone to get them out of the hot spot.

I said, "I'm sure that Miss Newman would like to wash up after the trip. Maybe Mary will show her to her room."

But Rourke wasn't going to let her off so easy. "Mary will stay right here," Rourke said. "People will be coming any time now. The family is to receive in the library. Forrester," she directed, "ring for Brooks to show Miss Newman to her room. Maguire, will you please get Russell out of there?" I stood my ground, Forrester pushed the button at the foot of the stairs. Rourke smiled at Sylvia Newman, a smile which declared open war. "I'm sure Forrester has told you all about us, Miss Newman, how eccentric we are. You have come at a very awkward time. I feel sorry for you. It won't be easy. Forrester should have had more sense than to subject you to this, but he isn't famous for doing the right thing at the right time."

Sylvia Newman returned the smile, the challenge. "You're nice to be concerned about me, Miss Donnelly, and perhaps you're wrong about Forrester. Perhaps this is the right thing at the right time."

Rourke took my arm suddenly, fondly, holding her face against my sleeve. "Maguire, here, is quite right. He understands women so well. Do go on upstairs and freshen up. I'll arrange for some sleeping pills. In case all this excitement has been too much for you, a short nap might revive you." The butler was standing ready. "Brooks, show Miss Newman to the Chinese Room." She turned and walked into the library before anyone could counterattack.

"Isn't she sweet?" I whispered.

"A doll. A living doll." Sylvia touched Forrester's cheek as she started upstairs. "Close your mouth, Forrester."

"I'm sorry, honey," he said. "Rourke is upset."

"Of course she is and I forgive her." She went upstairs rather majestically. Forrester shrugged his shoulders, Mary giggled and I went to get Russell away from the coffin.

"Hey, Russ. Break it up. You're missing all the fun." I poked him. "Come on. Your brother has brought home a real, live, red-blooded woman."

"Funny," he said. "It's as though I'm looking at myself. We do look alike, don't we?"

It was the first time I looked at the body, a waxy corpse, dried out and bloodless. I took hold of Russ and dragged him away. "Come on. The family is receiving in the library. It's almost time for the fireworks to begin."

"What's she like, Maguire?"

"Who?"

"Sonny's girl."

He played the same game on the hall floor, hopping from black square to black square. I, like a damn fool, hopped with him. "Between you and me? Promise you won't tell Rourke?" He nodded. "She's going to be rough to handle. She's an underprivileged

Rourke Donnelly, just as tough and just as smart and wants just as much."

"Damn it. I was hoping he would get someone who loved him. He needs to be loved."

"This one has got a needle in his arm, Russ. She's going to make a man out of him, hypo him into some kind of action."

"We'll have to stop her from hurting him, Maguire. We can't let her hurt him."

"Let's see what happens, Russ. Come on. There's the doorbell. You'd better line up for action."

CHAPTER FOUR

Rourke said she was not strong enough for a wake but that's what she had, a wake without tears and without food or drink. Except me. I made a few safaris into the kitchen, nipped from the bottle and raided the icebox. Most of the time I wandered through the crowd of whispering strangers looking for a familiar face, an encouraging smile. There were hundreds of people there and I was lonesome. Once I went upstairs, tried the door to the Chinese Room thinking I'd shoot the breeze with Sylvia Newman, but there was no answer to my knock and the door was locked.

Promptly at eleven o'clock, the men from the undertakers closed the parlor doors, whispered to the few remaining callers queued up to view the remains of Carleton Donnelly and they broke up, re-formed outside the library and filed through saying words of comfort to each of the children in turn. I parked myself in a dark corner of the room, closed my eyes and must have dozed off for a few minutes.

Russ woke me up with a gentle touch on the shoulder. "The show is over," he said. "Only the mourners remain."

Mary was curled up in a lounge chair, Rourke was in the wing chair by the fireplace. They both looked beat. Young Forrester had disappeared. I walked over and stood behind Rourke, touched her head. She drew away from me. "How did it go, Red?"

"Like clockwork," she said. "I could have written the script in advance. I knew what the governor would say and I knew the mayor would burp in the middle of a sentence. And poor Mat Lawrence. He was bursting to question me."

"Who's Mat Lawrence?" Russell asked.

"President of Forrester Steel," she answered. "All the presidents were bursting to ask questions. Waldron, Torrence and Davidson evidently didn't get into town yet. Tomorrow will be a mad day, you just watch."

Mary said, "Randy Lawrence is awfully attractive. He was so nice. He said such nice things. I haven't seen him in just years. He used to go to that awful fortnightly thing. He was good-looking even then. I think I would have given anything in the world if he had ever asked me to dance. He was older and so sophisticated and all the girls were absolutely goofy about him. He is attractive. His hair is turning gray a little right at the peak on his forehead."

"What did he say to you?" Rourke asked.

"He said he was sorry Father is dead."

"Anything else?"

"I don't see how it's any of your business, Rourke."

Rourke stood up, stood over Mary. "It makes a great deal of difference. Tell me exactly what he said to you. Every word."

Mary recoiled, curled up tighter. "I won't tell you. I just won't. It's personal. I don't have to tell you personal things."

"Damn it, Mary, I don't have time to play games with you. I'm tired and I'm fed up. Now tell me what he said."

Russ intercepted what could have developed into a hair-pulling contest. He did it quietly, walking between them, sitting on the floor in front of Mary's chair. "You don't always tell little personal things about yourself, Red," he smiled. "I remember once I tried to get you to tell me what you were doing with Charlie Woodward in the attic."

"Who the hell is Charlie Woodward?"

"You remember Charlie Woodward. Used to play halfback in high school. I caught you two in the attic once and you never would tell me what you were doing. Want to tell me now?"

"I don't even remember Charlie Woodward and what we were doing in the attic was none of your business then and it's none of your business now."

"Okay," he said. "I agree. I think Mary has the same privilege."

"Mary does not have the same privilege where business is concerned."

"He didn't say one thing about business," Mary interjected.

"Listen, Mary, Randy Lawrence and five hundred others like him are suddenly going to come to life now that Father is dead. They won't be after you. Remember that. They won't be after you, they'll be after money. Money grubbers. All of them. They won't want you because you're you, they'll want you because of your money. Free-loaders on a very high level."

Mary bit back her tears and drew her hand away from Russ who had taken it in a gesture of comfort. "You can't get me mad, Rourke. Not anymore. It doesn't matter what you say." She giggled nervously. "Wouldn't it be a scream if I should suddenly marry Randy Lawrence? Imagine Lois Barton's face. He was always her very special property. And Jean Stafford and Grace Fairley. All those girls. Imagine their faces if I should marry Randy Lawrence."

"Stop dreaming," Rourke commanded. "You will not marry Randy Lawrence. You will not marry anyone until we all agree he is the right man for you."

Mary folded her arms, stuck out her chin. "I'll marry who-ever I damn please."

Russell applauded softly.

Rourke said, "Now, listen to me, all of you. Stop playing these children's games. Normally I wouldn't give a damn what that drip of a Lawrence boy whispered into Mary's ear. I couldn't care less. But it's different with Father dead. There's the business to think of. Every casual word becomes important. Randy Lawrence isn't just Randy Lawrence. He's Mat Lawrence's son and he is Dexter

Cumming's nephew. Now do you understand why he was interested in you, Mary? Tell me exactly what he said."

Rourke had moved toward Mary, threateningly. Russell stood up quickly, still smiling. "Your Irish is showing, Red. It gives your face good color."

"Why don't you tell the real reason, Rourke," Mary cried. "Why don't you tell them what you're so frightened of. Why don't you talk about the will. Why don't you tell Russ that Father did not leave a last will and testament or if he did you never found it."

Russell said, "He must have left a will. He was a meticulous man. Meticulous men always leave a will."

"Of course he left a will. Mary doesn't know what she's talking about. He left a will and I did find it."

Mary jumped up. "What's in it, Rourke? Tell us what's in it. We have a right to know."

"Yes, Rourke, what *is* in Father's will?" Young Forrester was standing in the doorway to the library, standing straight up to his full height with Sylvia Newman's arm linked through his. The shut-eye Sylvia Newman had had gave her an advantage over the rest of us. She was fresh-looking, unlined and unharassed. Mary ran over to Forrester, linked her arm through his other arm. "Mary is right," he went on. "We have a right to know."

"You have a right to know nothing. Not any of you. Where were you when he needed you? Where were you when he was sick and dying and had to be helped like a baby. Or better yet, where were you when he wasn't sick, when you could have been here to enjoy him, work with him, learn from him?" She turned to Russell. "You were on a yacht or in bed with some tramp movie star. Does that give you a right? And you, Sonny, where were you?" She was right in front of young Forrester, flinging the words at him. "I'll tell you where you were; you were hiding out in a library, cringing in the stacks, afraid to come out and behave like a man, work like a man, meet your father on a man-to-man level. You're a great one, you are, all that Forrester blood in you boiling up … boiling up to nothing."

Mary spoke up. "Don't pick on them. Pick on me. Why don't you pick on me. I was here. I was here all the time. Did you ask for help? Did you even let me know he was sick? Did you give me a chance to be with him when he was dying?"

Rourke said, "Shut up, Mary."

"It's true," Mary went on. "She kept me away from Father. She kept everyone away from him. She wanted him all to herself. We're none of us to blame. You are, Rourke; you're to blame. You made us keep away from him, you made us stay away." She looked from Forrester to Russ. "Don't be afraid of her. Make her tell us what the will says. Make her tell us about the money."

"You're impossible, all of you." Rourke walked away, sat on the sofa. Russ followed her, sat down beside her, put his arm around her.

Forrester freed his arms of the women and stepped forward. "Mary is right, Rourke. What we were to Father was his doing and, in a way, your doing. But that isn't important now. We have a right to know about the will. If you know about it, we should know about it."

"Tomorrow," Rourke said. "We'll talk about it tomorrow. I've had enough tonight. Enough of all this … enough of all of you."

Young Forrester held his ground. "We want to know tonight."

"Well, you won't know tonight, Sonny. I'm not going to tell you. It's as simple as that. If you want reasons, I'll give them to you. First of all I'm so damn tired I could cry. Second, this is family business and you have chosen to bring in an outsider and I'm certain that Miss Goldman has no interest in our little family affairs."

"It's Newman, Rourke, and her first name is Sylvia and you'd better get used to it. We're going to get married."

Mary ran to her brother. "Oh, Sonny, I think it's just lovely." She kissed him. "I think it would be so wonderful if we can all find happiness now. I think it's just absolutely wonderful that you're going to get married."

Rourke stood up. "I'm going to bed."

"Aren't you going to wish us well, Rourke? Aren't you going to wish us happiness?"

When Rourke would not answer, Russell stood up and shook Forrester's hand. "I think it's great, kid. I think it's just what you need to make you happy." He walked over to Sylvia Newman, studied her for a moment, leaned forward to kiss her, aimed at her mouth. Expertly she turned her head so that his lips fell on her cheek. "Now that we've kissed," he said, "I think it's time for introductions. I'm the wayward brother."

"I'd know you anywhere," she said. "Forrester talks of you constantly. Thank you for your vote of confidence."

"We ought to have champagne," Mary said. "We ought to have champagne and drink a toast to Forrester and Sylvia and smash our glasses in the fireplace. Let's have champagne. Shall we have champagne?"

Russell's voice was quiet, soothing. "Later, Mary. When it's all over and we know who we are again. We'll drink champagne then."

Rourke started out of the room, her head down. At the door she almost collided with the butler, who was carrying a portable telephone. "There is a call for Mr. Maguire," he announced, then, finding me in the shadows, said, "Will you take it in here, sir?"

"Yeah, plug it in. I'll take it here." The children looked around at the sound of my voice. In the squabble they seemed to have forgotten that I was there on the fringe of their lives. Rourke kept walking, disappeared in the hall. Tactfully, Russ, Mary, Forrester and Sylvia drifted off to the other end of the room, circled in conversation. I took the phone and wondered who the hell knew I was holed up in the Forrester Mansion, as unlikely a place to find me as possible.

"John-boy?"

I did not recognize the man's voice. "Yeah?"

"It's Eddie Seguro. Where you been? Never see you around anymore. How goes it?"

"How did you find me, Eddie?"

"I got ways, boy. You know old Eddie; got an ear everywhere. Stay in touch, that's what I do. Never can tell when you've got to get hold of somebody fast."

"Spill it, Eddie. What's on your mind."

"Not so fast there. We're old pals, John-boy. Seems like a long time since we used to bum around together. Kids, we were. Crazy damn kids."

For a minute flashes of boyhood memories came back, the alleys, the tenements, the saloons, "Come on, Eddie, speak up. You're a busy man. You don't make small talk without a purpose. What do you want?"

"Same old Maguire. Old honest Abe. Come right to the point. No bulling around. All right, I want you to come over to my place. I'm having kind of a party. Got a fella here would like to see you, shoot the breeze. Matter of fact we're all set up waiting for you. I even have a car waiting for you. It's in the driveway of the Forrester place right now."

"Listen, Eddie, we've been through this before. Whatever kind of deal this is, I don't want any part of it. I thought I made that clear the last time. You don't need me. LaSalle Street is full of whipping boys to do your dirty work. Leave me clean, Eddie. Leave me alone."

"But this is a high-class deal. You don't think I'd get you in any of my regular crumb-bum deals. Not since you've moved up into high society. No, sir. This is a real high-class deal. I got to tell you, it's all way over my head. But this man here, he understands it and he's really anxious to talk to you."

"Forget it, Eddie. I'm not coming."

"Like I said, John-boy, there's a car waiting in the driveway. It's got a telephone in it. If you don't come out, those boys will come in and get you. Can I be any clearer than that?"

Eddie Seguro could be real clear. He had that reputation. He was not a man anybody spoke back to or said no to. I had said no once or twice and got away with it. But there was determination in his voice this time. "You mean this is come—or else?"

"Atta boy. You catch on real quick. Now, why don't you say good-by to all those high-class people and get in the car and come back to the old neighborhood for a little while, see how the other half lives."

"I know how you live, Eddie. I remember the old days in the old neighborhood. In those days you were a punk. In my book, you're still a punk. I'll get in the car and see your friend but that won't change anything. Is that coming through clear?"

He laughed. "I need you, John-boy. You're like a conscience to me. Whenever things get going too good, I ought to call you up and let you knock me down a peg or two. You're good for my character."

"All right. I'll be there."

"Ten minutes, John-boy. If you aren't out in ten minutes, in they come to get you. And you wouldn't be corny enough to try to beat it out a back door or window, would you?"

"Not me, Eddie. I'm no corn ball."

"I know that. High class. All the way through. Go right out the front door like a big shot, like a real society fella." He hung up quickly.

I wished I hadn't drunk so much or had slept more. Whatever it was that Eddie had on his mind would require me to be on my toes. But there was no way out. When Eddie threatened trouble he followed through. I mumbled my good nights to the clan and started out.

Russ caught up with me, talked in a low voice. "You're coming back tonight, aren't you?"

"I don't know. I've got an emergency case. A client wound up in the jug. It may take all night. I don't know."

"Try to get back. All hell is going to break loose here. We'll all need you."

"I'll try. You ought to turn in, Russ. You've been through a lot tonight."

He smiled, pleased with himself. "Funny thing is I don't even want a drink; I don't need one. I went through it all, all the callers and the family reunion, and I feel fine. I don't even want a drink. I may come through this in one piece."

"Good for you. Hang on."

"That Sylvia Newman is a bitch, isn't she?"

"So's your sister Rourke."

"Young Forrester is a nice boy, Maguire. We oughtn't to let him get fouled up."

"Tomorrow, Russ. We'll save him tomorrow. I got to get going."

The doors to the parlor were open. Rourke was standing at the casket. I checked my watch. I didn't have much time. When Eddie Seguro said ten minutes, he meant ten minutes. I went in, stood beside her, spoke her name. She turned to me, tears which she would not cry frosted her eyes. I took her into my arms gently, nuzzled the softness of her hair. "Baby," I whispered, "you've got your work cut out for you."

"Help me, Johnny. Help me." I didn't say anything. "You said you'd help and you didn't. You let them gang up on me. You let me forget how I wanted to be with them. Why can't I make them understand?"

"For the same reason they can't make you understand. I guess it's because you're all the way you are and that's it."

"You know why young Randy Lawrence was playing up to Mary, don't you? With Mary goes her block of stock right into the hands of Dexter Cummings. They're smart, all right. They know exactly what to do. They won't miss one trick."

"I got to go, Red."

"Where?" She stood back, looked hurt, deserted.

"Bail out a client."

"Come back tonight. You have to come back tonight. I mean we made a bargain. Brooks brought your clothes. You promised."

"As soon as I'm through I'll be back. It may not be until morning. But as soon as I'm through I'll be back." I put my arm around her and led her away from the coffin.

"Wait," she said. "I want to blow out the candles." She stood on tiptoe in front of the giant candelabrum, started blowing out the tapers. At the front door, I turned around just as the last candle flickered and went out. She was there in the darkness, alone with death . . . .

Two thugs were walking up the stairs as I came out. As I said, ten minutes was ten minutes to Eddie Seguro. They formed a bodyguard around me, escorted me down the walk to the street where a long, black Cadillac was waiting. I liked the fresh taste of the night air. I didn't even mind being sandwiched by these men or the prospect of facing Eddie Seguro. Rough as they all were, hoodlums and bums, they were my kind of people, people I understood and who understood me. I was outclassed with the Forrester-Donnelly clan, out of my league. This is what I understood, trigger men and Cadillacs with bullet-proof glass waiting at a curb, engine ready and running.

CHAPTER FIVE

He CADILLAC stopped finally in front of a warehouse in the stock yards district. Next to the door marked Office there was another door which led up a flight of frayed carpeted steps. At the landing, my heavy-set escort service pushed me through a door and into a small apartment. Funny about this apartment. Right away it smelled phony. At first I couldn't put my finger on what was wrong. The place had been furnished straight out of a Sears Roebuck catalogue complete to the wallpaper and the rabbit-ear antennae on the television set. It was a typical apartment for the area and for the income bracket of a guy who works around there. It was a real pleasant-looking place, mind you, but it was as phony-looking as a cigar stand fronting for a handbook operation.

A big man sat in a big chair watching the small television screen. He nodded toward the dining room. "They're in there," he said, running the words together. Deftly and firmly I was steered into the dining room, faced into a built-in china cabinet which suddenly swung open like a door. Beyond that bit of American borax was the kind of layout I expected Eddie Seguro to be shacked in.

This Eddie Seguro always had a taste for the lush and the exotic. His women ran that way, his ties ran that way, even his vocabulary fit into the picture. As soon as my feet sank into the plush striped carpeting, I felt better. This was the Eddie I knew, the Eddie I knew how to handle. There was a fountain in the room and mirrors so you couldn't tell where the floors ended and the walls began or which end was up. A Chinese-type tomato in native dress was throwing food to goldfish in the fountain. Usually I can take chop suey or leave it, but the straight sack dress she was wearing wasn't straight enough or sacky enough to hide what Eddie Seguro saw in this girl. It was plenty, well-proportioned for the area. One of the boys asked, "Where's Eddie?"

She kept feeding the fish and looking at me. Maybe to a Chinese girl an Irisher looks exotic. She didn't say anything, just kept sizing me up, measuring me with her slit eyes.

"Hey, where's Eddie?"

The girl looked away, back to the other fish. "He's in the library," she said.

The boys shouldered me forward. I held firm. "I'll wait here," I said. "Tell Eddie I'm waiting out here."

"You want to get your neck broke, mister?" the one with the boil on his nose asked. "This is fresh stuff. Hardly used at all. Eddie don't give nothing away until he's used it up real good."

"I'll wait here."

The thugs exchanged glances, went ahead and left me alone with the goldfish and the lotus blossom. I stood beside her, watched the fish snap up the crumbs she tossed them.

"You're looking for trouble," she said.

She was a little bit of a thing, didn't come anywhere near my shoulder. "Who's going to give me the trouble, you or him?"

"Him."

"Him I can handle. You I'm not so sure of. What's your name?"

"Chen Chan," she answered.

"You're kidding."

"Why?"

"I don't know. You don't expect Chinese girls to have Chinese names anymore."

Now she looked up at me, no expression on the doll face. "You have an Irish name and an Irish face."

"Been doing some research?"

"They've been talking about you in there."

"Good or bad?"

She shrugged her shoulders. "Both."

"Does Eddie ever let you out of this aquarium?"

"I don't want to leave. I like it here."

"Maybe you'd like it in the outside world."

"I've been there," she answered. "I like it here."

"Johnny-boy, Johnny-boy." It was Seguro clapping his hands and calling my name. "Good old Johnny-boy. Long time. Glad to see you, boy. Real glad you could make it tonight. I see you and Gladys are friends already."

"Gladys?"

Softly, she said, "My stage name is Chen Chan."

Seguro had one arm around Gladys and one arm around me. "He's an old friend, Gladys. Why, John-boy and I were kids together. I bet you wouldn't believe it. I bet you I'm no more than a couple years older than John. You keep yourself in shape." He punched my stomach and sent some of the Chinese butterflies scampering. "And you hold on to your hair. The clean life does it. Clean-living kid. That's the truth about him, Gladys. Always was a clean-living guy and a straight shooter, straight as an arrow."

"Okay, Eddie, let's get the alumni reunion over and get down to business."

"Right to the point. I like that. Right to the point." He put his arm through mine. "Excuse us, Gladys. Me and John has got some business to talk over." He led me down another corridor and through several vast and ridiculously extravagant rooms, all of them mirrored in the damnedest places and all of them filled with babbling brooks or fountains.

"Quite a layout, Eddie," I said. We were passing another aquarium. "How long have you been queer for goldfish?"

"Not me, John-boy. Hate the things. Got an interior decorator did this joint. Came all the way from New York. I said, take it away, give me the works, the sky's the limit. He was queer for goldfish, not me. And wait'll you see the library. Bought it right out of an English castle, the whole thing, walls, floor and books. You know who sat in my desk chair? The King of England. How do you like that, Eddie Seguro and the King of England using the same chair."

He was right about the library. It was a hell of a room. It even smelled right—old leather, hand-hewn logs, the damp smell of a poor heating system. It looked authentic to the last detail. The only anachronism besides Seguro was the stack of old racing forms piled up on a big oak table.

But the man who stood up as I came into the room belonged there. He was tall, this side of middle age, gray hair, good physical condition, quietly dressed and elegantly mannered. In the true man-of-distinction tradition he clutched an iceless highball, held out his other hand for me to shake. "I'm glad you came, Mr. Maguire," he said. "My name is Dexter Cummings."

It was only when our hands were clasped together that the name struck home. Everything made sense all at once. This was Dexter Cummings, the fabulous manipulator, the man who wanted the Forrester Industries and would stop at nothing to get them.

Seguro said, "I'll leave you boys alone to shoot the breeze. You want anything, just pull the cord."

When we were alone, I mixed myself a drink, swirled it over the ice and wondered if this day would ever end.

"Let me explain, Mr. Maguire, why I have asked you to meet me here," Cummings began.

"Look. Let's save time, huh? I know who you are and I know what you want."

"Fine," he said. "I like that. Do you also know what I'm prepared to pay?"

"No."

"Would you like to know?"

I thought about that and smiled. "You might give me a vague idea within a few hundred thousand dollars one way or the other."

"The price I am willing to pay is precisely one hundred thousand dollars."

I gave a long whistle.

"Yes," Cummings said. "One hundred thousand dollars is a great deal of money."

I looked at him and grinned in spite of myself. "What else is new?"

"One hundred thousand dollars," he repeated.

"There's a joke, Mr. Cummings, about a man who meets a beautiful woman for the first time and right off says, 'Will you go to bed with me for a hundred dollars.' She gets mad as hell and says, 'What do you think I am?' 'With any woman as beautiful as you, it's already established what you are. What we're discussing now is price.'"

Cummings did not crack a smile. "I don't haggle, Maguire. I've stated my deal. It's more money than you've ever seen or are likely to see at any one time."

"You missed the point of the story. I'm not a beautiful woman."

"But you have your price. Show me the man who doesn't."

I sat in Seguro's desk chair, where the King of England had sat. "Give me a little background music, Cummings. First of all, what do you think I can do? How do you think I can get you what you want?"

"I'll be honest with you, Mr. Maguire. There is no reason not to be. Until a few hours ago I didn't know you were alive. Suddenly Carleton Donnelly is dead. In the center of the confusion stands a stranger. The information I could get on you was meager. I know that you are in some kind of position of trust. The children trust you. Even Rourke, or maybe particularly Rourke. That I don't know yet. I don't know how they came to you or you to them. I know it's on a personal level, not legal. I've been able to check your legal background and it in no way indicates any contact on the level of the Forrester Industries."

"You put it politely," I said.

"I know this much. You are there and you are on the inside. You're in a position to give me information. You may even be in a position to influence things in my favor. I don't know the precise situation. I don't know what legal disposition Donnelly made of his controlling interest in the Forrester Industries. You may know and you may not. You may be in a position to find out. I know I need someone inside to give me information and to pass on information which I will give you. For this I will pay one hundred thousand dollars."

"You keep repeating that figure, Cummings. Kind of like a singing commercial." I leaned across the desk. "This may come as a big disappointment to you, but you've got the wrong boy. I don't mean anything to the Donnelly family and they don't mean anything to me. I'm an innocent bystander. If I took your money, it would be fraud."

"You're lying, Maguire. You're tied up with one of them or all of them. Rourke sent for you, I know that. She did it by telegram. I don't know the reason for that. You came to the house and were locked in a room with Rourke and then you spent a long time in Mary's room. You left the house and came back with Russ. You knew where to find him without any trouble and he knew you well enough and trusted you enough to come back home with you."

"You've got a pretty neat spy system, Mr. Cummings. Let me ask you something else. How does Eddie Seguro fit into this picture?"

"He fits nowhere. I have key people in key places who give me information I need quickly. No one in any of the usual channels knew you. So I tried the other end of the ladder. They didn't know you either. You weren't connected with big business or politics. You weren't known in your own profession. You weren't known in criminal circles. It was a fluke that Seguro knew you. You were kids together; as I understand it, you've had no business associations."

"I'm learning a hell of a lot about rich people today. You fellows have a marvelous gestapo system."

"Time is running out, Maguire. What's your answer?"

I didn't hurry to answer him. I looked around the room, ran my hand over the rich texture of the desk. "I've been in this spot before," I explained. "As a matter of fact Seguro put a deal to me once. It wasn't as polite as any of this and there wasn't as much money involved. But Eddie-boy wanted to use me. He wanted me to use someone else, betray trust someone had in me. So he put the deal up to me, not clean and straight the way you're doing. Eddie is a punk and he uses a punk's methods. He threatened me. You know, the boys would beat me up or a car might accidentally run over me or they'd fix my face so no dame would ever look twice at me. Incidentally, did you catch that Chinese dish Eddie's got himself? It's too good for him. Eddie's a punk."

Cummings stood across the desk, his hands on it firmly, looking fiercely down at me. "I am not a punk, Maguire."

"No. You're sure not a punk. If you were a punk I'd tell you what I told Eddie: to go screw yourself. But you're a high-class fellow, Mr. Dexter Cummings, and I don't know how to tell you to go screw yourself in a high-class way."

"That's your answer?"

I smiled. "I think I'll say it anyway. Go screw yourself, Cummings." I was pleased with the way I said it, real quiet-like. He was as red in the face as a man can be without having a heart attack. For a minute I thought he was going to make a lunge for me across the desk. But he turned and yanked at the bell cord next to the big stone fireplace. I expected the butler to show up with another drink, but Seguro's two henchmen stormed into the room, guns drawn, ready for trouble. Seguro followed them.

Somewhere in the background was the well-stacked lotus blossom, her face as impassive as an ivory carving. I leaned back in the King of England's chair and put my feet up on the Lord of Something's desk.

"Trouble?" Seguro asked.

Cummings said, "Tell them to put away those damn guns and get them out of here." Seguro made quick gestures with his head and the guns were back in their holsters and the dead-end boys were on their way out of the room. "Maguire will not listen to reason," Cummings explained to Seguro.

"I told you, Mr. Cummings. This boy don't figure at all. He don't make sense. What do you want to do?" Cummings began to pace; the tycoon was thinking. "You want rough stuff, Mr. Cummings, we got rough stuff. You want he should take a vacation on foreign shores for a while?" Seguro snapped his fingers. "It can be arranged. Whatever you want."

I stood up, walked around the desk. "Stop showing off, Eddie. You can't touch me."

"Don't be so sure, John-boy. Once I let you get away with it. I make mistakes, but only once do I make the same mistake." I started walking out the door. At the instant Eddie grabbed me, I chopped his hand away. "Where do you think you're going?" he said.

"I'm going out, Eddie. I'm going out and your boys are going to drive me back to the Forrester Mansion. This time they're going to all sit in the front seat and I'm going to sit in the back seat all by myself." I grabbed a liquor bottle off the tray. "I may even drink your Napoleon brandy on the way. I'll be careful not to spill any on the seat."

"You ain't going nowhere, Maguire."

"Sure I am, Eddie. I'm going and you want to know something else? If I wanted I could take that little bundle from the Chinese laundry right with me and you wouldn't stop me. Isn't that right, Mr. Cummings?" Cummings did not answer. "But I don't want her like that, Eddie. I want her when she comes to me of her own free will, when she gets tired of your slimy hands pawing her. Now call your boys and tell them I'm leaving. Tell them about the front seat."

Poor Eddie was bewildered. He turned to Cummings, his mouth open but speechless.

"Do as he says, Seguro," Cummings commanded. "Do everything as he says."

"But... I mean, I'm a big man here. I ain't going to let no two-bit lawyer..."

I interrupted him. "Not two-bit, Eddie. A three-hundred-thousand-dollar lawyer. That is what I am, isn't it, Mr. Cummings?"

There was hope in his face. He said, "It's already established what you are, Maguire; what we're discussing now is price."

I walked out on that line and rammed into my two big friends. "Go on in," I said. "Eddie has some instructions for you." I wandered through the maze of rooms until I found Chen Chan feeding other fish in another pond. "If you ever feel like slumming," I said, "you'll find the number of my fish bowl in the telephone book."

CHAPTER SIX

T HE LIGHT burned at the front door of the Forrester Mansion. There was this light and the light of the moon playing on the funeral wreath. The smell of the flowers flooded my nose as the picture of the bier came into my mind. I wanted to tell Eddie Seguro's driver to back up, get out of the driveway. I could go home now and still watch the late show, drink beer and watch the late show. Heaven. But I had promised them I would come back.

After leaning on the doorbell for a while, the butler opened the door. This faithful old family retainer was probably the leak to Dexter Cummings—him or one of the other servants. It didn't matter. There would be time enough to be careful tomorrow. "You're sleeping in the Dutch Room, Mr. Maguire. The bed is turned down. I wasn't able to find any pajamas or night shirt."

"I rough it at night. Just me and the sheets. Where do I find the Dutch Room?"

"At the head of the stairs, turn to the right. It's the third door on the left. You can't miss it. The door is split in half. The old Mr. Forrester brought it back from Holland."

"Good night. Thank you."

"Good night, Mr. Maguire."

I found the double-hung door without any trouble, opened both halves and went in. There was a big four-poster directly ahead. Russ lay on the bed, reading a book. He wore a too-tight sweatshirt; the stenciled *Boy's Latin School* across the chest had faded from many washings. "Sorry," I said. "I must have gotten in the wrong room."

"No, this is your room." He did not look up. "Mine connects through the bathroom. I've been waiting for you."

The room was paneled in a dark wood, filled with blue-and-white china gimcracks, tourist souvenirs of Holland. A replica of a windmill stood against one wall, the blades turning slowly like an electric fan in an old Southern hotel. "I'm tired as hell, Russ."

"Go take a shower. You'll feel better."

I started to undress. I was really beat. "Any hell break loose after I left?"

"Nothing much. Young Forrester's girl is still a bitch." He said it as a matter of fact, without feeling. He turned the page. "This is a hell of a book, you know that. *Tom Swift and His Airship.* Used to be real gone on Tom Swift. That's what I was going to be. All-American true blue. Man's man. Good to my mother. Only I never had a mother I knew."

"Did you tell your brother?"

"Tell him what?"

"That his girlfriend is a bitch?"

Russ put down the book, groped on the night table for a cigarette. "You have to understand about Sonny. You can't come right out and tell him about this broad. In a sense she's been good for him. She's built him up, given him confidence in himself. She pumped him up so that he thinks of himself as a man, not a pimply kid any more. She breathed some courage into him, or at least some spark which he thinks is courage. She's got his head clear and his pants hot. You can't tell a guy in that condition that his girl is a bitch. To him she's Joan of Arc and Eleanor Roosevelt all wrapped in a Marilyn Monroe package." I started for the bathroom. "You've got a pretty good build for a lawyer," Russ said. "You ought to watch the beer."

I touched my stomach where the muscles were beginning to get tired and give up. "What the hell," I said. I didn't know what else to say.

"Funny about the way I am," Russ said. "Nothing affects my body. It's as if it doesn't belong to me. I eat the wrong food and sometimes too much food and sometimes none at all. I drink too much and don't sleep enough. I wake up in beds I've never seen before. Nothing happens to me. I haven't changed a measurement since I was twenty-one. It's just inside that I'm rotting. Everything happens inside my head. All the filth and dissipation happens inside."

"Dorian Gray," I said.

"Like that," Russ answered. "Go take a shower."

It was an old-fashioned shower stall where the water comes at you from every direction, all sides, top and bottom. I let it run real hot and steaming. The pressure of the water was good; it hit hard and forced all thinking out of my brain. I was aware only of my body, the hot water hitting it and making it tingle, the steam relieving the tiredness in my bones and putting me in a kind of therapeutic coma. I coddled myself in the warm spray until I almost fell asleep on my feet. Then I shut off the hot water and turned on the cold full blast, cursed out loud and danced a jig as the icy water hit me.

One thing about rich people, they buy big bath towels, man-sized towels, rough and soft all at once. I rubbed myself hard until I was dry, helped myself to another towel and wrapped up in it, and went back into the bedroom. Russell pulled over a little to give me room.

"We had a man-to-man talk tonight," he said. "After you left, Sonny came to my room and we had a man-to-man talk."

"About what?"

"Life. Sex. Women. And you. He asked a lot of questions about you. He likes you, Maguire. He's caught the family fever for Maguire."

"I'm glad. He's a nice guy. I'd hate to see him get hurt."

Russ nodded. "It's going to happen. He's going to get hurt. He talked a lot about Sylvia Newman. He came right out and said what their plans were. He feels that being the only male descendant with Forrester blood, that control of the Forrester Industries by right belongs to him. He doesn't know the content of the will, but he seems to have boned up on some legal aspects of inheritance and inherent right. He has some classic legal examples cited where blood turned out thicker than water. I don't know enough about it to know if he makes sense or not. It doesn't matter. What is important is that he intends to fight Rourke or whoever else may be in his way. Young Forrester has decided that my father's mantle belongs to him and he's going to have it. He has great plans for what he's going to do when he becomes head of the Forrester Industries. It's going to be pro-labor management. He hopes eventually to build the structure so that at some point five or ten years from now he will turn over ownership to the employees, they will own their own company. He has a few classic examples of that, too, businesses being handed over to the workers. Funny thing about the kid, he's convincing. He has a lot of historical information to back him up. And he has a whole fund of social-science history dating from the Roosevelt era, stuff about similar developments in Scandinavia. Miss Newman must have supplied this information. She did a good job of selecting her facts. She has young Forrester indoctrinated all the way up to his ears."

"This is going to make a big hit with Rourke."

Russell laughed, and folded his arms behind his head. "He's not worried about fighting with Rourke. He has great confidence in everything he believes in. Come to think of it, this is the first time I've ever seen the kid happy, have a glow about anything. He has only one problem and that's what he really came to talk to me about. My authority seems to be limited to one field. It seems Miss Sylvia Newman isn't giving."

"That's a surprise."

"It's more than a surprise, Maguire. It's a damn lie. I can tell pretty well what kind of a woman she is. I can tell by the way she walks and the way she moves her mouth. Miss Newman needs it like she needs food and water. My guess is she needs it almost as regularly. She's giving, all right, but she isn't giving it to my brother. She's playing the virgin queen. She keeps the kid shivering in his trousers. She says no wedding, no hocus-pocus. His question to me was, now that they have announced their intent in front of the family, didn't I think he should be forceful with her, make her go to bed with him."

"What did you say?"

"You know what I said?" He laughed. "I told him he ought to respect the lady's wishes. I told him sex wasn't everything. I think I convinced him."

I yawned. "I got to catch some shut-eye, Russ. I'm beat."

"I haven't just been making small talk, Maguire. All this has a point. We have to save my brother from this Sylvia Newman."

"How do you expect to do that? You said yourself he was in no condition to listen to criticism of her."

"There's only one thing that will disillusion him. It's a dirty trick and I wouldn't like to do it unless it's absolutely necessary. It's going to hurt him like hell for a while, punch a big gaping hole in all this manliness he has acquired. It'll probably send him right back to school and the Middle Ages. But the way I figure it, there's no choice. Young Forrester has got to catch Miss Newman giving somebody else what she won't give him. What I've been thinking about is which one of us would be better. What do you think, Maguire? Who should bed her down, you or me?"

I had to laugh. With Russell Donnelly, the question and the answer was always sex. "She's a smart cookie," I warned. "She has a lot at stake. She'll be on her guard. What makes you think either one of us can get her into bed."

His smile was open, Tom Swift smiling at his airship. "There's not a doubt in my mind. Either one of us can make her. The question is will it hurt Sonny less if it's you or if it's me."

"Let's face it when the time comes, Russ. Go on to bed. I've got to get some sleep. Tomorrow may be worse than today." I pulled the towel off, turned back the covers and got under them. I leaned over to turn off the light. "Go on, Russ. We can talk about it tomorrow."

"Good night, old man," he said.

Poor Russ, I thought. How jazzed-up a guy can get, even a basically nice guy. I got to thinking about Rourke then, how much alike she and Russ were physically, the same cut of their bodies, the deceiving boyishness of the way Rourke was built. I dozed off thinking about that, seeing her in my mind's eye, aware that behind one of the doors in the darkened hall she too lay in bed. I wondered if she was thinking about me.

"Johnny."

It was in a dream and in the dream someone was calling my name.

"Johnny."

It was a dream and it was not a dream.

"Johnny."

I sat up in bed. Opened my eyes to the darkness. "Rourke," I said.

"No. It's Mary, Johnny. Were you asleep?"

"Yes. You ought not to be in here, Mary."

"I have to talk to you."

"Tomorrow, Mary. We'll talk tomorrow."

"You couldn't have been asleep very long. I knew Russ was in here. I heard him go back into his room." She moved forward. I reached over, turned on the light. She was wearing a pink robe. "Keep the light off, please. It'll be ever so much easier to talk in the dark. I used to be afraid of the dark. When I was a little girl I used to be afraid of the dark. But I like it now." I turned off the light. "There's a comfort in darkness; I can be all sorts of things in the dark that I wouldn't have the courage to be in the light. Have you ever felt that way?"

"I've never thought about it." That was a lie. I knew what she meant about darkness. I wished hard that she would leave. In the darkness she could be Rourke or Eddie Seguro's Chinese girl or the girl I had loved when I was sixteen. Darkness is a funny thing, it's made for dreams and for nightmares.

"I know you think I'm just awful and it would be terrible if anyone found me in here with you like this. But I just have to talk to you. I've tried to sleep but I just can't. If I wait until tomorrow I won't be able to say what I want to say. I have to say it tonight. Don't make me leave, Johnny. Please don't make me leave."

"All right, Mary." I lighted a cigarette. In the short flare of the match I saw her pale face and her glistening eyes. "Want a cigarette?"

"No, thank you." She sat on the edge of the bed timidly. "Weren't you proud of me tonight? Did you hear the way I spoke to Rourke, as if I wasn't afraid of her? I was trembling inside, I really was. At least part of me was. I was two people. I was the old Mary watching and listening to the new Mary. Does that sound silly? I mean does it sound silly to say you feel like two people at once. I feel that way now. I came here in the middle of the night and I know I shouldn't be here but something is just moving me, telling me what to do and I have no control over it. I don't know how to explain it."

"I understand."

She was silent then, framing words to say. She relaxed her weight on the bed. "It's going to be wonderful, isn't it, Johnny? I mean everything is going to be different for everybody. I'm so happy about Sonny. Don't you think Sylvia is stunning? So sophisticated! I don't think Rourke likes her but then you don't really expect Rourke to like anyone. She likes you, though. Tell me about it, Johnny. Tell me about you and Rourke. Do you love her very much?"

"I don't know, Mary. There hasn't been much time to be thinking about love."

"I can't wait to fall in love. I can't wait to be loved. What's it like, Johnny? What is love like?"

She lay beside me awkwardly, careful not to put her body in contact with mine. I was in a tough spot. "You must know what love is like," I said. "Songs are about love, books are about love."

"I don't mean that. I mean what it feels like in your heart. I mean..." She hesitated, stumbled. The words were hard to say. "I mean what is the act of love like?" Before I could answer, she giggled nervously. "You think I'm just awful, don't you? Some horrible kind of woman. I'm not. I don't mean to be. It's just that... well, I have to know what it's like, what is involved in love. I suppose it's terrible to ask you but there's no one else. I can't ask Rourke. She's not like a sister or even a mother. Rourke would laugh. Rourke would say I have no business wanting to know. She would say that loving is not for me." She moved closer, touching me now, tentatively, expecting to be pushed away. "And I can't ask Sonny. Sonny wouldn't know. He's as dumb as I am about love. I tried asking Russ once. He blushed. Isn't that funny, a man like Russ being embarrassed when I asked him about love."

"When you think about it," I said, "it isn't so funny."

"Are you embarrassed, Johnny? I mean I'm glad the lights are out because I must be blushing something dreadful and terrible welts come out on my forehead when I blush." She stopped talking abruptly. She had forced herself to say what she said, to ask the question. It was up to me now.

"Love," I said, "is a funny thing. The act of love is not always an act of love. It can be an act of violence, an act of boredom, an act of pity. It can be almost..."

"Do you pity me, Johnny?" she interrupted.

"No, Mary. I don't pity you at all. I envy you. You have it all ahead of you. The first time. That's always important, the first time. It scares you the first time. You stumble blindly and there is that awkward time when your mind is directing your actions. But then it's all right when the animal in you gets control. Then it's all right. The first time can be an important time."

Softly, she said, "There's never been a first time for me, Johnny."

"I know."

"I can't wait any longer, Johnny. I have to know. I have to feel it. I have to know for myself." She clutched at me in desperation. Her face was against mine, her hands grasping my shoulders. "Don't say no, Johnny. Don't say no."

I lay as motionless as I could as her hands ran over me. I was feeling a natural reaction to contact. I could give in to it, let the animal take control. And I was thinking that maybe I should. Mary was desperate. If it wasn't me, it would be someone else. Maybe it would be better with me. It had no meaning to me. I could be gentle with her, make the act of love an act of love. Then I reversed my thinking, knew I was out of my mind to consider it. It would put me in great shape with the family. And what if Rourke found out? But to turn Mary down would be tough on her. She was making her first try as a woman, and if I turned her down it could be disastrous for her. Then I was wondering what the hell ever happened to the old Maguire. The old Maguire figured a roll in the hay was a roll in hay and damn the consequences. Sure, I was thinking, that's the old Maguire, take what you can get when you can get it.

I took Mary into my arms, held her still. I could feel a flutter pass through her body. "Mary," I began, "the easiest thing in the world would be to make love to you now. Everything is right for it. It's tough to keep myself in check. But you can't talk about loving without talking about love. You're not the kind of girl, Mary, who will ever treat love lightly. There are some women who are like men in that sex means nothing to them beyond the physical act. It's something you do and it's great while it lasts and when it's over, it's over, and you forget it until the next time. But you're not like that, Mary. It won't be good for you unless your heart is tied up in it. Can you understand that? Sex without love is all right for someone like me. It's the best you can get, it's a release. But when you're in love, sex is maybe the greatest thing there is. I don't want to spoil that for you, Mary. You'll fall in love. There will be someone, and you'll fall in love. I want that to be the first time for you. He'll want it that way, too. Then it will be the greatest thing that ever happened to you. Wait for the right man. Then it isn't just an act of love. It's before, too, and after, and in-between. You understand that?" Her body recoiled in my arms, the way a flower closes against the chill of night. She drew away from me, got up from the bed. "Tell me you understand, Mary."

"Answer one question." Her voice was scarcely audible.

"What is it?"

"When I came in you thought it was Rourke. If it had been Rourke, would you have made love to her?"

There was no point in lying. "Yes," I said.

Mary began to cry. She bolted from the room, leaving the door open behind her.

I jumped out of bed, closed the door, closed the double latch, went into the bathroom, took a cold shower, got back into bed, and read three chapters of Tom Swift and His Airship before I finally fell asleep.

CHAPTER SEVEN

S TRONG SUNLIGHT pierced the Dutch Room. I felt it hot against my face, took my time about waking up. When I finally did, I reached over for my watch. It was ten o'clock. I jumped up fast, went into the bathroom, showered again and shaved. I opened the connecting door to Russell's room. His bed had not been slept in. Back in my own room, I dressed quickly. There was a knock at the door, and I released the latches. Rourke came in carrying a breakfast tray. A pencil was stuck in her hair and a notebook was tucked under her arm.

"It's about time you woke up, Maguire. Is this the time you usually go to work?"

I took the tray from her, set it on a table. "I had a hard night."

"With whom?" She nodded where the book had fallen to the floor. "Tom Swift give you trouble?"

"You seem very chipper this morning. Did you get all your problems solved?"

"Eat your breakfast. We have work to do." She sat down, thumbed through the notebook, jotted down a couple of notations. "You should see the flowers that were delivered here since eight o'clock this morning. Messages from all over the world. The editorials in the paper. The Donnelly family hasn't been this much in the news in years."

"How did you figure out your problems, Red."

"And how do you know I did?"

"You have that look about you. Supreme confidence. Everything under control."

Rourke laughed, and it was nice to watch her in the sunlight. She was warm and soft. "I've faced facts, Maguire. I have a logical mind so I used it. I was upset yesterday, off my usual pace. Nothing is different, no one is different. We're all the same as we always were. I will read Father's will. I will then tell the other children what we are going to do and then we will do it."

"Just like that, huh? No complications, no interference? What about the dragon lady?"

"Sylvia Newman? She can be handled easily. Money will get to her. And if money doesn't get to her I will recite a list which I had compiled, a list of subversive organizations to which Miss Newman has belonged since 1933."

"You may have a point. If I had a red record, I sure as hell would rather face a Congressional committee then have you put the screws on me."

"So I have arranged a family meeting at ten-thirty in the library. At eleven-thirty the Board of Control of the Forrester Industries will meet in the dining room. Luncheon will be served at twelve-thirty promptly. At two o'clock the house will be open for callers coming to view Father's remains. And you, Mr. Maguire, are cordially invited to all functions."

"If it's all the same to you, Red, I think I'll spend the morning back at my old stand chasing ambulances. You seem to have the situation well in hand. It looks like my tenure of service has expired."

"I'd like you to stay."

"What for?"

She fidgeted. "There could be a slip. We've all come to rather depend on you. Russ and I were talking this morning and we both thought it would be a good idea if we retained you permanently to ... well, to represent the family on a personal level. Obviously your legal background ... well, you understand that in a business way we're already very well represented by four large legal firms."

I wiped a dribble of eggs from my mouth. "I get it. You want me to be the old family retainer. Good old Uncle John. Come to him with all the personal-legal-type problems. It may not be a bad idea. I can handle things like driver's licenses, traffic tickets, dog licenses … It may not be such a bad deal."

"Please, Maguire. Try to understand. I'm asking you to stay because I need you. We all need you. Please stay."

"All right, Red. I'll stay and watch. I was just playing hard to get. As a matter of fact, you couldn't pry me away. You know what I think? I think there's going to be some fireworks." I finished my coffee. "Did you make the breakfast? I always said I never knew a girl who could fry eggs with so much authority."

"The cook made them. I admit I explained exactly how you like them. She's Irish. The name Maguire intrigued her."

"Red, I think you ought to know something about last night. I saw Dexter Cummings. That business call I got was from an old hoodlum buddy of mine. Not a buddy. I just have known him for a long time. Cummings found out about me, knew I was on the inside here. Then he found somebody who could get to me."

"How much did Dexter offer to pay you?"

"A hundred thousand dollars,'" I said.

"I hope you held out for more, Maguire. A hundred thousand dollars for control of the Forrester Industries is a steal. If you could deliver what Dexter wants, a million dollars wouldn't be too much. I hope you didn't sell out for less." Rourke was burning up inside.

"We're still haggling over the price. Thanks for the tip on what it's worth." I smiled. "You don't think I would consider making a deal, do you?"

"Why not? You have us under your particular brand of hypnosis. You can influence Russ and Mary and probably even Forrester. It wouldn't take much. You have no ties to us, no allegiance, no loyalty required. We are, after all, strangers to each other."

"You and me, Red? Strangers?"

"Why did you tell me about Dexter? Are you expecting a counter-offer from me? Dexter bids a hundred thousand, I bid two hundred thousand, he bids four and I bid five. Is that what you expect?"

"I guess I expected what I'm getting. I expected you to get sore, the color to come out on your face and those green eyes to give out with that old fire." I walked over, kissed her on the forehead. "You can relax, doll. I made no deal. As a matter of fact I told him to go screw himself, but I left him a wedge of hope, a very convenient wedge of hope. For two reasons I let it hang open. One, because if he thinks I'll do his dirty work for him, he might not try too hard to get at you in another way."

"You don't know Dexter. He'll stop at nothing."'

"You didn't let me finish. That's the second reason my refusal was not final. I knew that if Cummings was using Eddie Seguro he would stop at nothing, including roughing me up if I don't play ball. I was looking out for my skin, too. Eddie Seguro has been known to play dirty, even dirty enough for murder. When Eddie Seguro gets sore and someone stands in the way of his turning a buck, then Eddie Seguro can kill. Obviously, Seguro has made a deal with your blue-blooded friend. Seguro's job is to get me to play ball. I figure I want to live a little longer and as long as I'm alive I don't want my face mashed up or my legs broken. So I left the boys with a ray of hope."

"You're kidding, aren't you. You can't be serious. I know Dexter Cummings. Holy cow, I went to college with his sister. I used to go out with him. His family and my family belong to the same clubs. You can't tell me that Dexter would be mixed up in murder."

"You said he would stop at nothing to get the Forrester Industries."

"But not murder, not gangster tactics. He'd lie and bribe and cheat. He'd juggle the stock market and do dirty financial dealings, but not murder."

"For my sake, Red, I hope not. The important thing is that there is a nice big information leak from this house right to Mr. Cummings's well-brought-up ear. Like in the movies, I immediately suspect the butler. It could be someone else, a secretary or a maid, but on the basis of his information about me I think the butler did it."

"I can't believe it. Who could it be? Who would be in a position to know enough? It could be Brooks. Or perhaps Rosemary."

"Who's Rosemary?"

"A girl who does typing and stenographic work. But she doesn't know you. I don't think she's even seen you."

"I have a real good way of finding out. I'll call Cummings and ask him." I took the phone on the desk. "What's his telephone number?"

"You're not serious. You don't think he'll tell you?"

"Sure he will. Do you know his telephone number?"

"Try the stock exchange. He'll probably be around there." I began to dial the number she gave me. "You have a fat chance of getting Dexter to tell you who the spy is."

"You forget, Red, that a man's mind is different from a woman's. Most men aren't petty." I went through a series of offices and a coterie of secretaries before I got to the secretary closest to Mr. Cummings. She gave me the brush-off. "Look," I told the girl, "you tell Mr. Cummings that Mr. Maguire is on the line. If he won't talk to me, then I'll go quietly and leave you to fend off the next intruder."

"You'll have to tell me what it is that you wish to talk to Mr. Cummings about. Just what is the nature of your business, Mr. Maguire?"

"I'm a procurer. He asked me to get a girl for him. Now, get him on the line."

It was a few minutes, then Cummings voice. "Glad to hear from you, Maguire. I was just thinking about you."

"That's nice. I was thinking about you too."

"You're ready to make a deal?"

"Well, I don't know. All I know is all night long the figure of two hundred thousand dollars kept buzzing around in my head."

"You must have been dreaming," Cummings said. "In real life the amount was one hundred thousand dollars."

"The reason I called is that somebody in this house is getting information to you. I felt it only right to tell Rourke about it. I didn't want it on my conscience. Also, in case I take this case for you, I don't want any internal competition. We've tried to figure out which one of the employees it could be. My candidate is the butler. But Rourke pointed out that it could be any of the servants on the office staff. Rourke's only solution is to fire them all, clear out the house entirely of the hired help and get new ones. I admit it's a foolproof method, but a lot of innocent heads are going to get cut off in the process. I told Rourke that if I explained the situation, told you a lot of people were going to be thrown out of work and your source of information would be cut off in any case, that you would tell me who the spy is and save the innocent."

"You understand, Maguire, that even if you do know who my employee is there, you can take no legal action. There has been no technical crime committed."

"It's understood and agreed."

Cummings said, "You'd make a good detective. It is the butler. When Rourke discharges him, have her tell him to come to my office and I'll pay him off."

"Thanks, old man, I knew you were a gentleman."

"You might call me after the family conference and the reading of the will. I think you'll have time before the Board of Control meeting. I'll know about what happens at the meeting. My brother-in-law is a director, you know."

"We'll take special care of him, make sure the new butler doesn't spill soup on him."

"I'll hear from you later?"

"I wouldn't be surprised, Mr. Cummings." I hung up. "Like I said, the butler did it."

"The dirty bastard," Rourke commented. "I'll have to call Gapers and have them send an extra butler with the staff to serve luncheon." She made the proper notation in her notebook. "What else did Dexter say?"

"He said you should tell Brooks to collect his money at Dexter's office."

"Did he say how much stock he was able to buy? The stock is going down fast. I'm buying as much as I can. When Dexter starts bidding it up it's going to climb right back to where it was, higher even." She eared her pencil. "I've got to fly. I have a million and one things to do before the family conclave." She hesitated at the door. "Mary's gone back into her shell. She's locked in again and she's crying. I've sent Russ to try to snap her out of it. You'd think just once in their lives they could behave like grown-up people." She was out the door, then back again quickly. "We're putting you through a lot, Maguire. Above and beyond," she said. "Don't be concerned about the financial compensation."

"I'm not worried about that, Red. I'm worried about why I didn't get a big wet kiss this morning."

She smiled slowly, lowered her head. "I tried, Maguire, but your door was locked." She was gone again, with a slam of the double-hung door.

I dialed the number of my secretarial answering service. The assistant, a girl named Gwen, answered. I disguised my voice. "Mr. John Maguire, please."

"Just one moment, I'll ring his office." (Pause.) "I'm sorry, Mr. Maguire is in conference, may I have him call you back."

"May I speak to his secretary, please."

"His secretary? Just a moment, please." I could see Gwen holding her hand over the telephone, look across the desk to Tina and give her that signal of desperation.

"Mr. Maguire's office." It was Tina's voice, calm and clear, just as regular as the Sunday paper.

"Hello, doll."

"Well if it isn't his eminence. What's on your mind, buddy? I have no time for former lovers this morning."

"Current, doll. Very current. Anxious for you this very minute."

"I bet."

"Don't be sore, Tina. You know it has to be something big to make me miss your goulash."

"Something big? You mean like a size-D cup? I know you long, hard and well, buddy, and I have had it. I looked in the mirror this morning and had a long heart-to-heart with myself. I examined the little lines around my eyes and the little shadows around my mouth and made a large decision. The decision includes you out. Way out. Like in left field or all the way out of the ball park. Somewhere on Addison Street. 'Bye."

"This was honest-to-goodness business."

"Sure, it was. One of those all-night conferences. You want to know something? I don't care. I am now one Tina Weston, woman of action. At twelve-thirty today I am having lunch with Mr. Parsons. You know Mr. Parsons, the one who is so crazy about me. It's about time for him to ask me to marry him. If he's on schedule, today is the day. I'm going to make him eat a hearty lunch because when he asks me today, I'm going to say yes and it's liable to surprise him so much he'll faint."

"Maybe he'll just throw up like he did at the last Christmas party."

"Make fun of him if you want, Mr. Maguire, but he's going to be mine, all mine. Such as he is, he'll be all mine." She waited a minute. "Can you top that?"

"Tina, listen to me. I know you're mad. I know I give you a bad time. But you also know how it is with me. I'm not the steady, settle-down-and-get-married type."

She forced a yawn and said, "I've noticed."

"If Parsons was any kind of a real guy, a guy I thought would make you happy, a guy good enough for you, I'd say go ahead and give you my blessings. But Parsons. Holy cow—" and as I said it, I thought of Rourke—"not poor little Parsons. He won't last one round with you."

"I'm bored, Mr. Maguire. Would you like your messages?"

"Go ahead."

"Two ugly gentlemen with concealed weapons called on you and are now hovering outside your office door. A Mrs. Gallagher called and said the landlord decided not to evict her. A man named Harry Foster called, no message. A Miss Chen Chan called, no message. The telephone company called about your listing in the new classified directory. I asked them if they had a classification for tomcats but unfortunately you would have to be listed under domestic animals."

"Ha, ha, ha."

"Is there anything else?"

"Yeah. Don't marry Mr. Parsons. And if you want to reach me and it's urgent, call Whitehall 6-0800 but don't give the number to anyone at all. You don't even know where I am."

"Look, save me the trouble of calling Whitehall 6-2080 and getting the listing for Whitehall 6-0800."

"The phone is unlisted," I said. "Bawdy houses never give out any information." Tina hung up and I smiled. She had threatened me with Mr. Parsons before. It didn't mean anything. But just in case, I called a friend of mine in Cicero, a guy who owns a lumber yard. He owed me a favor. Then I called Mr. Parsons, gave him a song and dance about a good case which I couldn't handle, told him the man had to see him at twelve o'clock sharp, gave him the address in Cicero. It's a long trip by streetcar to Cicero, just as long coming back. Tina would cool off by then.

⚜ ⚜ ⚜

It sounded like a cat hissing but it was Sylvia Newman calling to me from the Chinese Room. I stepped into the chamber of Chinese horrors. My room looked like something in a modern motel compared to where they had installed Miss Newman. "Grotesque, isn't it," she said. "Rourke's idea of a joke. And you can just leave that door open, Mr. Maguire. We can talk softly."

"And carry a big stick?"

"Don't brag, Mr. Maguire. Sit down and listen to me." I sat down in one dragon-covered chair which broke my back and invaded the seat of my trousers. I tried two more, gave up finally and sat on the floor. "I am not included in the family meeting this morning," she said. "I understand that you are." I nodded. "Forrester was all for making an issue of it but I decided against it."

"A wise decision."

She smiled, showing a good set of teeth. "You know Forrester thinks very well of you, Mr. Maguire. He's only seen you fleetingly but he likes your manner, the way you seem to understand the peculiar relationship of the Donnelly family. I confess that I rather like you, too. I trust you to do the right thing."

"This whole flight into high society is going to give me a swelled head. Everybody trusts me. It's dandy to be such a trusted friend to man and beast."

"You and I can talk the same language. I would like to give you a briefing on the situation with Forrester Donnelly and his position in regard to the Forrester Industries."

I interrupted. "If we're going to talk the same language, doll, let's talk it. I need no briefing. You and young Forrester want control of the Industries."

"Do you know the content of Carleton Donnelly's will?"

"In about ten minutes, everyone is going to know the content of Carleton Donnelly's will."

"But you know it now."

"What's the difference?"

"The difference is that I think we can prove that Forrester's father was ill for many months, desperately ill, and in the last month, helpless. He could have been coerced in his decisions, undue influence exerted. There have been cases before when ..."

I got up. "Save it, cookie, until you need it. You'll get nowhere with me. I don't know anything. The will could have been written ten years ago, twenty years ago when he was hale and hearty. Relax until you know what you've got to fight."

"All right, Mr. Maguire. Just let me say one thing. If this all works out to Forrester's benefit, it will also work out to your benefit. You have my word on that."

"You know something, Russell is right about you. You'd be sensational in the hay."

Miss Newman gave me that Theda Bara smile. "Likewise, I'm sure," she said. And I was thinking Russ was right about a lot of things.

I got almost to the staircase but Russ stopped me as he came out of Mary's room. "She told me what happened," Russ said. "You shouldn't have done it, Maguire. I thought you understood about Mary, how she's constructed emotionally."

"What do you mean, I shouldn't have done it? I didn't do it. If she's crying, she's crying because I didn't do it. Either way she would be crying."

"I'm sorry, old man, I know you didn't touch her. What I'm saying is that you should have. I mean this kid is busting with it. You would have been good for her. Hell, it wouldn't have meant anything to a man like you. You're like me. But it would have meant everything to Mary. She'd be all alive now, blooming."

I shook my head. "You've got it figured wrong. Mary isn't that kind of girl, Russ. She's the kind who would hate herself in the morning, worse than she hates me right now."

"She doesn't hate you, she's ashamed. She's ashamed of herself, ashamed to face you. I've been talking to her for an hour and

I can't get anywhere. I've tried everything. I've told her all the times it's happened to me."

"How many times?" I laughed.

"Once," he said. "Maybe twice." He thought for a moment, shook his head. "No, only once."

"I'll go in and talk to her," I said.

"She told me how you let her down gently, how you explained to her about...well, how it has meaning when you're in love. You're right about that, Maguire. It's something I've known all along without knowing it in words. It's what's wrong with me, maybe. I keep looking for it. Woman after woman. It's never bad but it's never as good as it should be.... You know what I mean, like the full blast of the greatest symphony orchestra in the world. So you try to kick it up, hypo it with liquor and dope and tricks. But that doesn't work. And you go from woman to woman hoping each time a new one will make it like that, the full power of the symphony. No good. But *you* hit it right on the head. Without love, it isn't what it should be."

"I don't like hearing the story of my life," I said.

"You, too?" He smiled. "Too bad about us. Too bad we weren't caught, married young. You know, catch the morning train seven-forty A.M. and home on the five-twenty P.M. Then one night you stay late, figure you'll take the nine-thirty P.M. and the girl who takes dictation comes in and one thing leads to another. That has a zing to it because you're cheating; it's kicked up because there's the danger of being caught. Too bad we aren't like other guys."

If I had been smart, I would have walked out right then, straight down the stairs, out the front door and into a saloon, get roaring drunk, have a hell of a fight and pick up a girl to heal my wounds. They were getting to me. The Donnelly clan was getting to me, scratching through the surfaces I'd spent my life building up around myself. The hell with this baring of souls, stirring up of feelings I'd like to leave unfelt. A man like me lives from day to day, does what he can to make his way in the world, takes what fun he can get and sleeps a good sleep at night. I couldn't be that man as long as I stayed in this house. They were getting to me, all of them, each in his own little way. I should have walked right out, but Mary was crying so I went in to her, sat on the bed, touched her hair.

There were so many words to say and Russ had probably said them all. Words were no good. I took her by the shoulders, sat her up so that she faced me. Her eyes looked away. I held her chin and I kissed her, this was no brotherly kind of kiss, it was a kiss I had kissed before, mechanical, skillful, the way a whore kisses. She was cold to it at first, but she gave in to it then. It was a long kiss and it did the job it had to do. Mary came alive, and all the trapped feeling inside her body tried to pour out of her mouth— frantic, inept lips, tongue and teeth. I broke away and smiled at her, open-faced and honest-abe. Now I was Tom Swift. I was Tom Swift promising to become Errol Flynn. Mary smiled back at me, looked at me. I winked, touched her face, took her hand and led her down the stairs. When I passed the stain-glass window I made a motionless sign of the cross and said a few silent words. I felt like an awful shit.

The Donnelly children had assumed their normal positions. Rourke was ramrod in the wing chair. She had pulled a table in front of her and spread papers out on it. Russ was horizontal on the leather couch, his shoes off, his tie open, his eyes shut. Young Forrester was unrelaxed in a chair built for relaxing. Mary went right over to Russ, curled up on the floor next to the sofa. I retreated to my dark corner.

The library was a morbid room even in daylight. The windows were leaded and stained a smoke color. The heavy draperies decreased the light even more. Some of the flowers had been set up in here and they were wilting almost perceptibly. It was an awkward time and the silence was awkward and the way Rourke shuffled the papers was awkward and when she finally spoke, her voice sounded hollow, far away, at the other end of a stone vault.

"Father wrote his last will and testament three years ago. The exact date is June fifteenth. It was witnessed by Mary Hathway and Grace George. They were both employees of the Forrester Industries. I've checked to see where they are now. Miss Hathway died last year and Grace George is in an asylum in Iowa."

"Let that be a lesson," Russell said, "to anyone who wants to work for the Forrester Industries."

"The will is all perfectly legal,'" Rourke went on. "Even though Father wrote it himself and his attorneys did not see it or know about it, it is valid. He followed a form of an earlier will he had made, which the lawyers still have a copy of. I've checked this with old Mr. Peachum. I did not tell him the content of the will, I only checked to see if such a handwritten will would be legal. It is."

Mary fidgeted. "Get on with it, Rourke. Read it."

Rourke cleared her throat, picked up a piece of paper. "I, Carleton Donnelly, of Chicago, Illinois, being of sound and disposing mind, memory and ..."

Russ jumped up, bumping into Mary. "Wait a minute, Red," he said. He went to the fireplace, flicked the switch which lighted the portrait of Dolly Forrester. He smiled, a small boy smiling at the completion of a trick of magic. He ran his index finger over the corner of the frame, testing it for dust. Then he resumed his place on the couch.

"I, Carleton Donnelly, of Chicago, Illinois, being of sound and disposing mind, memory and understanding, hereby make, ordain, publish and declare this to be my last Will and Testament; and I hereby revoke all ..."

Now young Forrester interrupted. "We can skip over all that legal stuff, Rourke. Just read the business things."

"There is very little," Rourke said. "There is a section on taxes and stuff. He made a few bequests to some of the office people; John Brott, for one, is left five thousand dollars. He's the service superintendent at the Forrester Building."

"Hey, Sonny, do you remember him?" Russ rolled over on his stomach and looked at his brother. "He was the old guy with the square beard who kept telling us he used to be a sea captain. Remember the time he rode us up and down the freight elevator and it got stuck between floors and we were both so scared except old John told us all those stories about sailing to the South Seas and looking for secret treasure. I wonder if they were true, the things he told us. Like Samoa. How he was captured by the natives in Samoa and they..."

"Stop it, Russ. Stop it." Rourke's voice was edged with tension.

Russell rolled over on his back, muttered, "It was probably all lies. He made them up so we wouldn't get scared being stuck in the elevator like that."

"I'd better read this paragraph," Rourke went on. "It was in the first will, too. 'I hereby direct that on the plot of ground held in my name in the Calvary Cemetery, Atlanta, Georgia, a pillar of stone be erected so that it is at least three feet higher than the monument standing on the adjoining plot which carries the name Christopher John Rourke, and that my name shall be chiseled into this stone pillar. For this purpose a sum of twenty thousand dollars is bequeathed for the erection of the monument and the perpetual care of the plot.'"

"We can go there now, Red. He'd never let us go to Atlanta." Russell was in a self-induced trance. "We can go now and see our mother's grave. In all the ways I defied him, that was one thing I could never do. I never went to Atlanta and stood over my mother's grave. It was a kid's dream. Remember, Red, you had it, too. We used to daydream it together. We would go to Atlanta and stand over our mother's grave and we'd each shed one tear. It's a hell of a thing to know you killed a woman getting yourself born. But we can go there now. Just you and me, Red. We'll go before they put up the monument to him. We'll stand there in the middle of the graves of the Rourke family." He sat up quickly, fired with a new idea. "Hey, Red, when you went through his stuff, did you find it? Did you?" Rourke shook her head. Some of his mood had penetrated to her, caught her in his daydream. "We'll look later. There has to be a picture, a lock of hair. There has to be something. It's terrible not knowing what your own mother looked like. We used to argue about that, remember? To me she was always a lady in a white dress, all billowy and stuff. And she had yellow hair and blue, blue eyes. Remember the time we fought so hard and he caught us and made us tell what the fight was about. Oh, how he blew his stack that day! We were both punished. Even you, Red. He even punished you. When I think back on it, you were right, I guess. She must have looked like you. Red hair, green eyes. She looked like you. That could be the reason he felt the way he did about you. No." He shook his head. "No, I was right. You looked like him. She must have been different, something very special. Maybe she had black hair and violet eyes. That's a wonderful combination. Black hair and violet eyes."

Young Forrester spoke softly, sympathetically but with authority. "I think we ought to get on with the reading of the will."

To no one in particular, Russell said, "Violet eyes."

"This is the important paragraph: 'I hereby direct that all my earthly possessions, cash, bonds, stocks, real estate notes, etc. be divided equally among my four children, namely, Rourke, Russell, Forrester and Mary.'" Not one of the children moved nor did their faces betray an emotion. "'Particular attention is directed to the controlling interest of the Forrester Industries held in my name. This holding is to be divided into four equal shares but I specifically direct that my children decide which one of them will represent these holdings on the Board of Control of the Forrester Industries. In the event that they cannot decide within five days of my death which one of them will take control of the Industries, then it is specifically directed that all stock held in my name be sold to the public and the monies acquired become part of the estate.'" Rourke hesitated, cleared her throat again. "There're more legal paragraphs but in essence that is what Father wants us to do."

Russell said, "The old son of a bitch." He said it quietly, to no one. "I can't understand why he included me. I don't get it. There's a trick to it somewhere, something I don't understand."

"I think it's lovely," Mary said. "We're all so rich now. Money of our own. It's such a lovely, lovely will."

They all turned to look at Forrester and measure his reaction. He was silent, his face still without emotion. Rourke said, "It's a different will than I would have expected. I didn't think he would relent about Russ."

"He didn't relent." Russ was sitting up. "That's the gimmick. He didn't relent. He wouldn't forgive me. Not for any reason would he soften up. This is another punishment. In his own weird way, he doped this out as another punishment for me. I wish I could see through it; I wish I could look ahead and figure how this is going to bring disaster to me."

"Can't you just believe that he wanted you to have the money, that he felt you had a right to your share. Why do you all make him out such an ogre? He was more than fair. He was more fair to all of you than you had any right to expect."

Now Forrester spoke up. His face was serious, the blemishes of his skin heavier and redder. "What you mean is that he was less fair to you. That is what you mean, isn't it, Rourke?"

Rourke was caught off guard for a moment but quickly gained control of herself. "Yes, that is what I mean. Why should I be ashamed of it? It wasn't any of you who stood by him, worked with him, nursed him. It wasn't any of you. I did it alone. Certainly I think I was entitled to a bigger share than you. I worked for it and I deserved it. But Father did not feel that way. We were all his children and he wanted us to share it equally. I'm disappointed, naturally, but I have even greater respect for Father than I did before. I love him more because he was man enough to sacrifice his own feelings to do what he thought was the honorable and fair thing to do."

"I think you're right, Rourke," Mary said. "It was a lovely thing to do, share it equally. It makes me feel almost ashamed of the things I was thinking about, the way my imagination ran wild when I thought about how the money would be divided up. You know something? This is the first nice thing he ever did for me. The very first nice thing. It is the first thing he ever gave me that I didn't have to cry for or plead for. The first and last nice thing he ever did."

"Don't be too sure, Mary," Russell warned. "I still think he had a trick behind his thinking, some kind of a gigantic practical joke to make us all more miserable and Rourke more important."

"It's obvious," Forrester began. "Russ is right. It must be a gigantic plot. In the thirteenth century there was a man named William of Wolstein, a feudal lord with four sons, all of whom he hated. Unlike Father, he did not wait until he died to watch his master plan unfold. He divided his lands in four parts, one quarter to each son. He lived out his old age watching his sons steal from each other, war against each other, and finally destroy each other. What Father has done is not unlike that."

Mary was churlish. "You're being silly, Sonny. What Father has done isn't like that at all. How can we destroy each other? Even if we can't agree on who is going to run the Industries, the worst that can happen is everything is sold. But we still get the money."

"You're right, Sonny. You're absolutely right. The old son of a bitch. You have to respect him." Russ tapped his own head. "The boy had a real genius for getting what he wanted." He stood up, began walking around, fired up with the understanding which was coming to him. "It's very simple. Obviously the money is not important. The money divided by four is still more money than I could ever spend in my lifetime, or piddle away or throw away. The money isn't part of it. He only wanted to show us one thing. He wanted to show us that Rourke is better than we are. He left the four of us to fight it out, knowing damn well Rourke would beat us down, get her way, run the show. And Rourke's winning would be like his winning, giving us one more licking, one more feel of that iron hand of his. That's the gimmick, Sonny. Not that we will destroy each other, but that Rourke will destroy us again. One more time for him to whip us into submission. The last, last laugh."

Mary couldn't believe it. "Oh, he wouldn't, Russ. Why would he? I mean we all know that... well, I mean all we really care about is the money. Rourke is the only one who cares about the Industries." Mary put out her hand, touched Russell's leg. "I mean that... well, you know how we all love you, Russ, but you don't know anything about business. You don't even care. You live with all those glamorous people, do those glamorous things. You certainly wouldn't want to have anything to do with the Industries. And I certainly wouldn't. It's too silly to even think about. And there we are. There isn't any question, unless..." Her voice trailed off as she turned her head and looked at Forrester. "Golly, Sonny, you wouldn't... You have your school and your studies. You've always wanted to be a professor or something. Edit that Journal. You sent me one once all about people and places I never heard of. That's what you want, isn't it? You don't want this, do you?"

They waited for young Forrester to say something, but he didn't answer. I was watching Rourke, trying to detect her frame of mind, her plan of action. She had expected this, so she must be prepared. She was sitting calmly, waiting. They were both waiting, Forrester and Rourke, both playing the same game. They were letting Russ and Mary do the talking for them.

Russ walked over to his younger brother, "Look, old man, I don't know what you're thinking. You've got the Forrester name, and this is essentially Forrester money."

"It started out Forrester money," young Forrester said. "But the money has grown, snowballed into amounts so vast that I don't think Grandpa Forrester ever dreamed of that kind of empire. Father was partially responsible for that. The times he lived in had a great deal to do with it, too. But you can't deny Father's brilliance in business. You can discredit his methods, his means to gain his own end, but you cannot discredit the results of his handling of the Industries. I'm a Forrester, and I'm a Donnelly, too. I can see both sides of it."

Mary said, "Why do we always have to take sides? All my life, ever since I can remember, whenever anything happened we had to take sides. There wasn't ever a time when all four of us were on the same side, when all wanted the same thing. I think it's just awful that we have to take sides against each other. Why can't we all want the same thing at the same time?"

"We're not made that way, Mary." Russ smiled at her. "We're made to be the way we are. A messy lot, I admit. But we are what we are."

"I don't think that's true anymore," Forrester said. "I'm not what I used to be."

Russell took the bait. "Don't fool yourself, Sonny. We don't change. We've been carefully molded to be what we are. You think you're different, Sonny, because you've got a girl who makes sense to you, who talks sense and backs up her intuition with some carefully edited facts. Don't delude yourself, kid. And don't let her delude you."

"You mean Sylvia?" Russ nodded. "Let's get this straight, Russ," Forrester said. "I love Sylvia and I'm going to marry her. That's an unedited fact. I won't deny that she's been a big influence on me. She's brought me out of my shell, taught me to know myself, know what I am and what I can do. Perhaps you're right,

Russ; none of us ever changes. If you are, then I was always the way I am now. It's been buried under a lot of history and history books, but it was there all the time. Otherwise I couldn't be what I am now."

"But you're letting this woman make you something you never wanted to be."

"Watch out, Russ. Don't get me mad. I think I love you as much as I love anyone. I know all your faults and I know all the great things about you, the kind of wisdom you have. But don't say anything against Sylvia. Never, Russ. I may be mixed up about a lot of things but I'm clear about her and what she means to me."

"Look, kid, I don't mean it the way it sounds. Hell, I'm no one to preach about women or anything else. I'm sorry, Sonny. I shot off my damn mouth and I'm sorry. And what I want most in the world is a drink." He turned to me in my corner, and all the others' eyes turned to me too, surprised to find that I was still there on the edge of things. "Hey, Maguire, do you think you can scare up a drink? I need it. We could all use a drink." Then back to his brother. "Sonny, if I ever talk like that again, slug me. I have no right. Of all the people in the world, I have the least right to tell anyone else how to live his life. I'm sorry."

"Forget it, Russ."

"How about that drink, Maguire? Good idea, huh?"

"It's a lousy idea," I said. "You have a lot to talk out, and a Board of Control to have lunch with. Get over the hump, Russ. Don't give in."

Russell laughed, put a shaking hand to his forehead. He was perspiring heavily, his skin glistening with sweat. "I like your friend, Rourke." He cocked his head toward me. "Your friend Maguire is a great big Irish conscience for me. Keeps me in line. Maybe if I lie down for a minute—" He was unsteady. I stood up ready to help him, but Mary and Young Forrester supported him on either side, led him back to the couch where he lay down.

Mary took a handkerchief and wiped his face, then held his hand as she sat on the floor again. Forrester retreated to his chair.

"If you're all quite through," Rourke said, "with the self-analysis and remembrances of things past, I would like to bring up a few important facts. First of all, as Maguire pointed out, the men from the Industries are joining us for lunch. They will expect to know the substantial content of the will and they will expect to know who will take Father's place as the chairman and director of the entire operation."

"We have five days," Forrester said.

"We don't have five days. The market was flooded this morning with small stockholders dumping Forrester stock. I've been buying what I can. The important thing to remember is that as much stock as possible must be kept in the family. Dexter Cummings is also buying as much as he can. He wants control of the Industries. He wants it so much he'll go to any means to get it. You can ask Maguire. He'll tell you how far Cummings is prepared to go." They all looked at me. I didn't say anything. "Cummings will never get control as long as we stick together. Mary was right. We never have all been on the same side. Now we have to be. If we aren't together, we'll lose everything that belongs to us."

"But not the money, Rourke. We'll still get the money."

"Not quite, Mary," Rourke explained. "If we are forced to sell our stock, the price of it will go way down. It won't be worth what it was yesterday or what it will be worth a week from now if we all stick together."

"But there will still be plenty of money, won't there, Rourke?"

"That isn't the point, Mary. The point at this moment is that we are prepared to walk into that meeting and speak as a family unit. We tell them what will happen. We tell the Board what is going to be done—they don't tell us. Is that clear?"

"Why don't we save time, Rourke, and discuss the big problem," Forrester said. "Who's going to represent us? Which one of us is going in to say he is the head of the family, the head of the Industries?"

"There can't be any question about it, Sonny. You know that. None of you is the least bit familiar with the operation. Don't forget the Industries have been my life. I've sacrificed my life for the moment when someone would have to take over and know what to do. I'm not complaining. I knew what I was doing. I did it willingly. No one forced me."

"That isn't true," Forrester said. "We forced you. Russell and I forced you by being the way we were. If either of us had shown any interest, if either of us had pitched in the way you did. If either of us ..."

"But you didn't, Sonny. Neither of you. We're not dealing with *ifs;* we're dealing with cold facts. The fact is that you did not and I did. I know what to do now, and no one else does. The Board will accept me, they'll have to. They know damn well that Father trained me for this; this is what Father wanted."

Forrester did not let up. He was handling himself well, calm and self-assured. "The will said that Father wanted us—the four of us—to decide which one would take over. If Father wanted you he would have named you."

"You heard Russ's analysis. He's probably right. This may have been a trick of Father's to let us get in a fight because he knew I would have to win, once and for all. Actually I think he planned beyond what Russ said. If he had handed me the control in his will, the rest of you would have resented it. This way there can be no doubt. This has to be decided on the basis of qualification. I am the qualified one."

"Maybe so, Rourke, but I think in the long haul I can do a better job than you."

"You can do a better job? Have you lost your sanity, Sonny? What are you thinking about? What would happen if we walked into those men and announced that you were taking over? They'd laugh us all out of there. Those men know me. They'll look to me for the answer. What do you expect me to say—my little brother is taking over? It's ridiculous, Sonny. It's more than ridiculous; it's ludicrous. What does that woman do, feed you dope? Are you hopped up with marijuana? Remember who you are, Sonny. Just remember who you are."

"I know who I am, Rourke. I didn't know it for a long time, but I know it now. Let's try not to get mad at each other. You and I never fought, Rourke. I always stayed out of your way. I don't think you even know me very well. You ought to give me a chance. You might even get to like me."

"Liking you has nothing to do with anything," Rourke said.

"Try looking at this from another point of view, Rourke. It's the good thing about having studied history. It gives you a point of view. Look at it this way. Why wouldn't it be logical for the only male Forrester heir to take over? I think it's what people would expect. They are the Forrester Industries, founded by Simon Forrester, developed by Carleton Donnelly. My name is Forrester Donnelly. It makes sense from that standpoint, from the standpoint that I have historical right."

"If you had thought of this ten years ago or even five years ago, Sonny, everything might be different. But this is pretty late in the game to suddenly try to live up to your namesake heritage,"

"And you know damn well, Rourke, ten years ago, or five years ago, I wouldn't have had a chance. Father would have broken me in little pieces. You and Father together. I'm glad I waited. It's the smartest thing I ever did. If I had tried five years ago I wouldn't have had a chance."

"You don't have a chance now, Sonny. Not a chance in the world. I'd let it all go to hell before I'd give my consent to letting you run the Forrester Industries."

Forrester stood up, came over to Rourke, smiled at her. This kid had blood in his eye and yet there was a tenderness about him. You could see that he had feeling for Rourke, a kind of love. He was trying to be a big brother now, not a little one. "I'm not a fool, Rourke. I know I don't know much about the Industries, but I know more than you think. These last months I've been boning up on the operation of the businesses. I don't say I know as much as you do about them. I don't know a fraction of what you know. But you and I are not mutually exclusive, Rourke. We're brother and sister. We can work as a team. You can teach me. I'll learn fast, I promise you that."

"Do you think I'm going to take all the years I've put in, all the experience and the knowledge I've sweated for and hand it to you on a platter? Don't be a fool, Sonny, and don't play me for a sentimental slob."

"I don't deny anything you say. I know how you've worked. I know how important you were to Father." Forrester pulled up a chair, sat close to her. "I also know what you gave up. I know the men you could have had, the life you could have had. Kids, and everything. You missed all that, and I blame myself for it. But it's not too late, Rourke. You're not too old to have those things now."

"Don't be impertinent, Sonny."

"It's true," Mary said. "You could have had so many men. So many wonderful men were in love with you, Rourke. I used to dream about your wedding. I was the maid of honor and I wore pale, pale blue. It was a beautiful wedding, Rourke. You looked so lovely, so very beautiful."

"You have a right," Forrester went on, "to some personal happiness. You have a right to a life of your own. You have a right to be able to be in love and be concerned about only that one man and making him happy." He made a deliberate gesture of turning to me and smiling sadly. "It's a man's job you're trying to do. It's my job, Rourke. I'll need you to help me, but I can do it. It won't take long and then you'll be free to do what you please, live a woman's life. I know I'm right, Rourke. It's tough for you to see it now but you will." Rourke had begun to laugh to herself, a soundless laughter in the middle of bewilderment. Forrester turned to Russell. "Don't you think I'm right, Russ? Don't you think that Rourke has the right to be a woman, live a woman's life?"

Russell looked at the ceiling. "You know what I think? I think this is all a lot of conversation for nothing. I think Rourke has a right to live a woman's life, but she doesn't want it. She wants the Forrester Industries. She wants to run the whole shebang and make it more than it is today—vaster, richer, greater. She doesn't want a house in the country, a station wagon, a husband and kids. She wants the Forrester Industries."

"Are you taking her side against mine?" Forrester asked.

"I'm taking nobody's side. Not yet. I'm telling the truth about Rourke. I know her all the way I know myself. Better, even. She doesn't want the soft, gentle things in life. She wants the tough stuff, the stuff the Forrester Industries are made of."

Rourke stood up. "You're damn right I do, Russ. I want what the Forrester Industries are made of. And I can do a hell of a job with them. I *have* done a hell of a job with them. I've started expansion programs which have increased the power of the Industries. I've started bringing the business up to date. That's what I want. You're damn right, Russ. You have me pegged just right. No house in the country, no station wagon, no husband, no children."

"It's a damn shame, Red," Russ said. "It's a damn shame what Father did to you. Maybe, after all, you got the worst deal from him. Maybe his love loused up your life more than his hate loused up ours."

"Don't feel sorry for me. Don't any of you feel sorry for me. Feel sorry for yourselves that you're such miserable, weak specimens. I get what I want."

"Not this time," Forrester said.

"This time, Sonny. I'm going into that meeting and announce that the family has decided that I'm going to take Father's place. I'll tell them what is going to happen, how the show will be run." She brushed past Forrester, heading for the door.

"If you do, Rourke, I speak up. I'll tell them the real content of the will. I'll tell them that the decision has to be unanimous to be legal. I'll tell them it is not unanimous." Forrester was keeping careful control of himself as he spoke. Every word took great conscious effort. It was the diligence of a paralytic learning to walk again. "I'll tell them the truth, Rourke."

"You wouldn't dare!"

"Don't dare him, Red," Russ warned. "I think he will."

Forrester didn't reaffirm his stand in words, but he looked like a man of determination. Rourke stared at him, wide-eyed and unbelieving.

This was the time for me. This was the season for courageous men. I've faced guns without shaking inside. I've fought three guys at a clip without batting an eyelash. But this took guts, a kind of guts I wasn't accustomed to using.

I stood up and came forward into the center of the stage. "Red, you wanted me here; you asked me to stay. The rest of you did, too. I'm going to speak my piece as a lawyer. Any objections?" No one spoke, so I kept going. "Your Father's will gives you five days to reach a unanimous decision. You have no legal right to go in there, Red, and tell those men that a decision has been made. There are many considerations here, problems which no one of you has considered. There is no reason to tell the Board anything today. You have a right as mourners to put off any business discussions until at least after the funeral. You have five days. Take that much time if you need it."

"You know what time means, Maguire," Rourke said. "Time means time for Dexter Cummings, time for him to pull us apart more than we are. Look at what he's doing. He sent that sniveling nephew of his to court Mary. He offered you a bribe, a big one, if you'll give him the information he needs to take control of the Industries. Just wait until Dexter Cummings finds out the contents of the will. He'll keep us fighting each other until we have to relinquish all the stock; then he'll buy what he needs to take over. Time can only be on Cummings's side. I have to be able to announce to the newspapers this afternoon that the Donnelly family is sticking together, that we're acting as a unit to retain the control of the Industries."

"You can't do it, Red. You can't do it according to the conditions of the will."

"Are you going to turn against me too, Maguire? Are you on their side? I don't care. I'll fight you too if it's necessary. You don't scare me. You've let them get to you, my dear brothers and sisters. They've cried and bellyached themselves so that you feel sorry for them and think I'm taking frightful advantage of them. I thought you were a man, Maguire. If you were a man, you'd recognize a man. Do you see one here? Is he one?" She pointed at Russ, then to Forrester. "Or is he?"

"You listen to me, Red. You hired me as a lawyer."

"Well, damn it," she shouted, "you're fired."

"I don't fire so easy. You asked for this. I got my rear end in a sling for you and I'm not leaving now."

"Bravo." Russ applauded. "If she fires you, Maguire, I'll hire you. I'm loaded with dough now. Name your fee."

"I'll hire you, too," Mary said. "We'll make you rich."

"I don't want to be rich. I'll tell you all right now I'm not taking one damn cent from any of you. I'll send the estate a bill for what I usually get. Maybe I'll add fifty bucks for extra mental anguish. I think I'm entitled. But forget money now. You've got to go in and eat lunch with the Board of Control. Now get in there and act like bereaved children. Don't one of you talk business, any kind of business. Talk about your father; say what you want about him. If they ask you point-blank about the will, say it hasn't been read yet, you don't know what's in it. Rourke is right. You have to act as a family unit. I don't think any of you wants to let the control get out of the family's hands. By fighting each other that is exactly what is going to happen. Fight in private, work it out behind locked doors, but don't air it in the dining room."

"That makes sense to me," Forrester said.

"Russ?" He nodded his approval. "Mary?" She smiled and shook her head. "That leaves you, Red. Will you go along with this?"

"I hate you, Maguire. I hate you for taking their side against mine."

"I'm not taking anyone's side. You know that."

"If it weren't for you, I would have announced the family's decision. Sonny wouldn't have dared cross me. You don't know him the way I do. He's jelly, Maguire. If you hadn't opened your big Irish trap, it would have worked out my way."

"But I did open my big Irish trap, and you try any tricks in that dining room and I'll open it again before Forrester has a chance to open his. Do I make myself clear?"

"You make yourself very clear." She turned to the others. "You see what he's doing, don't you? You know what he is. He's a two-bit shyster lawyer. He's got a deal with Dexter Cummings. You know why he wants time? He wants time to close his deal with Cummings, double-cross us completely. I once said my father would have liked you, Maguire. I was wrong. My father was smarter than I. He would have recognized you instantly for what you are, a cheap ambulance chaser, a guy on the make for a fast fortune." Back to the children. "Can't you see he plotted this, how he's tricked you and deceived you? Look at yourself, Mary, goo-goo eyes in love with him. And what is he to you, Russ? He's your Alcoholics Anonymous, he's your character, as you said, your conscience. And you, Sonny. Yesterday you talked to me to make sure Maguire would stick around. What do you need him for? You need his muscles to back up this new man you think you've become. Can't you all see how he's played with you, worked himself into your confidence so he can use you to get what he wants. Can't you see that?"

"I asked you a question, Red. I asked you if you agreed to keep your mouth shut in there. I'm not asking any more. I'm telling you to keep your mouth shut or I'll push those pretty teeth down that lovely throat."

Rourke turned and stormed out of the room. After a minute Mary followed her, and then Forrester, looking too damn smug to suit me. Finally Russ moved his body from the sofa, took my arm and started to walk with me. "She didn't really mean it," he said. "You know that, don't you?"

"I'm not a big man for slugging broads," I said. "But I came close."

"She would have loved it, Maguire. Might be just the thing she needs. If the situation comes around again, slug her."

"She'll slug me back," I said.

Russ agreed. "Might be the beginning of something beautiful between you."

"You got yourself a hell of a girl for a sister."

"Too bad," he said. "I mean too bad she's my sister. Otherwise she's just my type."

CHAPTER EIGHT

S SOON AS we were in the front hall, the new butler snagged
me. "Mr. Maguire, a young lady has called repeatedly for
you. She left a message for you to call your office as soon as the
meeting was over. She asked that I interrupt the meeting, but
Miss Donnelly left explicit instructions that under no circumstances was anyone to come into the library. I trust I did the right
thing, sir."

"Sure, you did fine." The children had gone into the parlor,
where the directors of the Industries were in small, soft-spoken
clusters. But it was the body of Carleton Donnelly which domi-
nated the room, his dead presence, his posthumous power. I
ducked back into the library and called my office.

Tina answered. "What have you been doing? This telephone
has been jingling like a June bride. What gives, Counselor?
What's with this everybody being hot for John Maguire's body?"

"I'm desirable, that's all. Incidentally, how come you're
in there now? I thought you had a big lunch date with love in
bloom."

"I changed my mind. I canceled my date."

"It must have broken poor Mr. Parson' heart. I can just see
him now, dejected in the men's room."

"Let's can the small talk, Counselor. An unidentified man
has called every ten minutes on the ten minutes. A frantic lady
named Miss Chan has been calling on the alternate ten minutes. A man named Eddie Seguro called just once, but he made
up in threats what he lacks in quantity of phone calls. You are

to call him at Yards 8-6090. Miss Chan's number is Chow Mein 3-7969. Oh, pardon me, that exchange is Wentworth. What else is new?"

"I'm crazy about you and I'm glad you threw Mr. Parsons over."

"Will you marry me?"

"Hell, no," I said.

"Drop dead, Counselor." She hung up.

I started dialing Seguro's number when a man walked into the library and closed the door behind him. I dropped the receiver back on the cradle. "We haven't met yet," he said, extending his hand. "My name is Mathew Lawrence. I'm head of Forrester Steel."

We shook hands. "Glad to see you, Mr. Lawrence. My name is John Maguire."

"Oh, we all know about you, Mr. Maguire. News gets around very quickly. That Rourke is a sly one. She works so hard you'd never guess she would have time." He clapped his hands together. "Well, I suppose, after a decent period of mourning, you two will tie the old knot, huh?"

"I think you have me figured wrong, Mr. Lawrence. I am retained as legal counsel to the family."

He nudged me and winked. "But we can talk man to man, can't we, Maguire? We know the way of the world." He sat down, crossed his legs with difficulty. His fat stomach was in the way. "You met my brother-in-law last night."

"Eddie Seguro."

"No. No, not him. You know who I mean."

"Then it must be Mr. Cummings. Yes, I met him last night."

"Bright boy. Got a lot of the old noodle. He used to be the little brother I could buy off with a nickel for a candy bar or an ice cream cone. It doesn't seem possible what he is now."

"I don't know what he is now, Mr. Lawrence, but it sure as hell takes more than a nickel to buy him off."

"Dex told me this morning that he had had a little chat with you. Said you were stubborn. I spoke up to Dex. I really did. I told him he was going at this thing the wrong way. It isn't like Dex to use strong-arm methods to get what he wants. I told him he was all wrong in his approach to this thing. I told him I'd have a chat with you, talk on your own level, none of this hoodlum stuff. I've known Rourke since she was a little girl. I think I saw her not more than a year or so after Carleton brought the kids up from Atlanta. Pretty little thing. She was a spitfire even then. I watched that girl grow up. I always felt sorry for her, being under the eye of Carleton all the time. I'm not telling any tales out of school when I say that Donnelly was not an easy man to get along with. He was tough, hard as nails. He had rigid standards and he imposed them on everyone who worked for him, Rourke most of all. He was a strict father, a hard taskmaster. Rourke had so many opportunities to live a wonderful life. You know, there was a time when Dexter Cummings and Rourke were … well, that way about each other. But her father smashed that romance, claimed Dexter was a fortune hunter, a no-good. Dexter never got over that, and never got over Rourke. It may be responsible for his success today. I think when Donnelly broke up the romance, Dexter vowed to get even, to smash Donnelly's power just as Donnelly had taken everything away from old Simon Forrester."

"I didn't know about Rourke and Dexter Cummings."

"No, I didn't suppose you would. It's a forbidden subject around this house. The scandal is over and forgotten. I think everyone has forgotten except Dex and maybe Rourke. You must have known that there were some men in Rourke's life. She's a beautiful woman, and with beautiful women there are always men."

"It explains a lot," I said.

"Then I'm glad I told you. It does explain a lot, but it doesn't help anything. Dexter is still what he is and Rourke is still what she is and the Industries can't help but suffer because of it. That's what I told Dex last night. I told him maybe he was continuing a war that no one wanted to fight any more. With you in the picture I thought things would be different. Rourke wouldn't be interested in the business, not with you around. I told Dex, with her father out of the picture, she'd be free of the ball and chain, she'd be free to be in love, get married and live like any other woman. Her father would never let her do that. The way I see it is that you'll sit in on the Board in an advisory capacity and throw the ball back to us, the individual presidents who make up the Board. I'll be honest with you, it means a lot to me personally. I'm the senior president. If it's up to the Board, I'll be elected chairman and be put in nominal control. Rourke trusts me, I think. She knows I'll do the right thing. Of course there will have to be some stock adjustment; the family will have to release some of their shares to us at the going rate."

"I think it's premature to talk about this, Mr. Lawrence. I think you ought to give the children a chance to bury their father before you force them into business decisions."

Lawrence went right on, ignoring my interruption. "This whole plan is contingent, I suppose, on any specific requests Carleton Donnelly might have as to the disposition of stock in the Industries. I know that will has just been read and I thought you could shed some light on the legal aspects of this so that I can adjust my thinking accordingly."

"Everyone, no matter how fancy he talks, gets back to the same question. The question is what the will says, what was Mr. Donnelly's last request for the disposition of his stock. Your bright brother-in-law offered me a lot of money for that information, Mr. Lawrence, and I turned him down cold. You have asked me on a gentleman-to-gentleman basis. I'm not having any of that either."

"You realize, Mr. Maguire, that my association with my brother-in-law is very close. If I fail in my method to win you over to my way of thinking I will have to abandon you to his way of thinking. Do you understand?"

"If what you're trying to say is that Mr. Cummings is planning on enlisting the heavy hand of Mr. Seguro to make me talk, then I understand very well. I also think it would be a great idea if you get out of here before I get mad."

He struggled to his feet. "You're something different around this house, a new note. You remind me of Carleton when he first came here from Atlanta. Yes, of course, that's it. You're even built like him. You have that same arrogance, that cock-sure attitude and the same raw fists. He had Dolly Forrester and you have Rourke Donnelly. My brother-in-law was right again. You are a man to be reckoned with, Mr. Maguire. The Forrester Industries has another Irish tough guy to beat his way to the top. Good luck, Mr. Maguire. Remember one thing—we have experience behind us now. We've always said, those of us on the Board, that we would know how to deal with another Carleton Donnelly if one should come along."

Lawrence collided head-on with a steaming Rourke. "Just stay where you are, Mat," she said. "I want to talk to you."

"Want me to leave, Red?"

"No, stick around, Maguire. I'd like to hear the deal Lawrence made. I think I should have the opportunity to outbid him."

Mathew Lawrence smiled. "Maybe you can talk some sense into him, Rourke. He doesn't listen to reason. If you love him at all, you won't want to see him hurt. Dex is out for blood this time. I'm against his tactics but you know I never carry any weight where Dex is concerned. Have a talk with your friend, Rourke. I'd hate to see him get into trouble."

"The hell with Maguire right now. Why did you bring Randy here? Since when is your son a member of the Board of Directors?"

"He didn't come in that capacity. Randy came to see Mary. He was taken with her last night. I guess they used to know each other when they were kids. He came to see Mary. I said it was all right. I knew it wouldn't matter to you, just one more place at the lunch table."

"You don't think for one minute that I don't see through you and your precious Randy. I know what you're up to. It won't do you any good, and it will only make poor Mary unhappy. You have no right to do that, Mat. Mary's had a hellish enough life without your planting Randy to hurt her even more."

Lawrence shook his head sadly. "You wouldn't believe me if I told you that this wasn't my doing, would you, Rourke? You wouldn't believe me if I told you Randy was really attracted to Mary, feels sorry for her, wants to be with her now?"

"You know damn well I wouldn't believe it."

"Will lunch be ready soon? I'm getting hungry." Lawrence walked out and left me with my tiger.

Rourke walked in an aimless circle. "I don't know how to begin," she said.

"You don't have to begin anywhere. You're sorry, I know that. And you think I'm right about the will. It's okay. I forgive you; I understand you."

"It's so damn hard being all things to all people. It was a mistake dragging you into this. You confuse me terribly. I keep feeling things I shouldn't at the oddest times, just because you're here. You're so God-awful wrong about so many things and so right about other things. I don't know what I am with you. I can't be Rourke Donnelly and the woman in Wisconsin all at once."

"It's a pity you can't be."

"Is it?" She stopped in the middle of the circle. She nodded her head. "Yes, it is a pity. It's a damn shame. But that's the way it is."

"It's okay, Red. I understand about you."

"And I understand about you, Maguire, and why you had to speak up the way you did. I could kill you for it, but I understand. I guess I even respect you for it."

"Should we kiss and make up?"

Rourke smiled. "That's the first good idea you've had today."

And during that kiss everything else was nonexistent, beyond the limits of our awareness. I had to think about love. This wasn't any kiss with any girl. This was what Russ had talked about, the full sound of a symphony orchestra, music you hear with your ears and feel in your stomach, your whole body rocking with vibration of it. When you feel that, you have to think about love.

"Maguire," she whispered.

"Don't do that to my ear, it tickles." She kept doing it, to my great pleasure.

"Maguire."

"Huh?"

"Are you really in danger. Was Mat serious about Dexter's plans?"

"I suppose. I can take care of myself. I've lasted, so far."

"I'm worried."

"Good."

"No, I'm serious."

"So am I," I kissed her again.

She broke off this time. "Holy cow! Now I have to rearrange the whole table because of Randy Lawrence. Damn it, I wish Mat hadn't brought him. I'm serious about his hurting Mary. Well, I'll fix that. I won't sit him next to her."

"If it'll do any good I'll duck out to a hamburger stand for lunch.

"Not on your life. You are sitting next to the dragon lady."

"Sylvia Newman? Thank you. We'll probably play sideways kneesy under the table."

"Can you imagine what the Board will say when they get a load of her?"

"If there's a good whistle left in one of them, she'll draw whistles, not words."

"Do you really think she's attractive?"

"Jealous?"

"Not a bit. Curious is all. I just wondered if you like the exotic type."

This reminded me that Miss Chen Chan was waiting breathless at a telephone for me, as was Mr. Eddie Seguro. I pushed Rourke out to rearrange place cards and I called the number Eddie had left.

"John-boy, glad you called back. We're having a little meeting today, two-thirty here at my place. The boys will pick you up at two-fifteen."

"I'm not having any, Eddie. No dice. The situation has not changed since last night."

"The boys will be there, John-boy. You don't want to embarrass your swell friends with any rough stuff, do you? Be ready at two-fifteen. The boys will come in and get you. They'd better find you there, lover, or there's going to be an unfortunate incident in the Forrester Mansion, completely covered by all the local newspapers. It's a bad time for unfavorable publicity. Agreed, Johnny?"

"All right, Eddie. The fresh air will probably do me good. But don't expect anything. As I said, the situation hasn't changed since last night."

"My friend Mr. Cummings thinks things will be different. Don't disappoint him."

And that was that with Mr. Seguro. Things were different with Miss Chen Chan. "I took a day off," she purred.

"Good for you."

"Do you want to come up to my place or should I come up to yours?"

"Just like that?"

"Isn't that what you want?"

I tried to see her the way I saw her last night, tried to work up that itchy feeling I had about her, but the taste of Rourke's mouth was too fresh. "Look, doll, I'm tied up in a big deal. You know, major-league stuff. I'd give anything to kick it around tonight, but I don't think I can break away. I'll tell you what—if I can shake loose, I'll give you a call. But don't hold up anything on account of me. If you don't answer your telephone, I'll understand. I'll try again."

"I'll be here," she said.

"I'll try."

I went to the john, washed my hands, then made my entrance into the dining room. Everyone else was already seated. Rourke made a general introduction and I took my place between Mary and the dragon lady. It was a lousy lunch, luke-warm food, hushed conversations, Mary playing footsy with me on one side and the dragon lady playing kneesy on the other. Tomorrow I was going to have lunch at the YMCA.

CHAPTER NINE

FELT BETTER for it. My eye was cut and my nose was bleeding some, my knuckles were raw but I felt better for it. Eddie Seguro had used up two guys on me. One of them lay unconscious at the other end of the room, the other sat on the floor, a bloody pulp. Eddie was holding a gun, but that didn't scare me any. He was too smart to use it.

"You had me figured wrong," I said. I was breathing hard. "Trouble with you, punk, is you don't remember the good old days well enough. If you had remembered when we were kids together you would have known you were at least one guy short. It takes two to hold me and one to slug me. That's three, Eddie, and you only had two. I know you didn't count yourself. This dirty work is all behind you now."

"You're right, John-boy. I forgot how tough you were. I figured the years had maybe softened you up some. I got to hand it to you." He kept the gun steady as he sat down. "As long as. you didn't respond to that treatment, maybe you got more respect for a gun." He released the safety. "You must know that I have a very good reputation with a gun. This is your last chance, Johnny. Give with the information. I'm getting tired playing games with you."

"Don't scare me, Eddie. You wouldn't use that on me. You're too smart. You're past the stage of being a trigger man. You're a big man now, an operator. Operators don't use guns, and especially not in their own apartments."

"You're not using your noodle, Maguire. There's big dough riding on this. No peanuts. Big, big dough. Even for my kind of guy, this is big dough and for big dough the boss has got to step in even if it means pulling the trigger himself." He looked around him. "And there couldn't be a safer place to knock off a guy than in this apartment. Soundproof, the whole thing. Very few people even know that this joint is here. Only my friends know and I got loyal friends, Johnny. And downstairs we got a small blast furnace, do some steel work down there. It's as easy as pie to dump a body. One big flame … and no evidence. Be smart, John-boy. Talk. Talk a lot. It'll mean dough for you, too. Big dough. We can both be rich."

The sitting gorilla had pulled himself to his feet and was getting up enough steam to rush me again. "You going to tell him to lay off or should I kiss him good this time?"

"Kiss him good. The bum has got it coming to him."

In a blind rage, the man rushed me. I let him have it good, swiftly and neatly, just as I learned in the old neighborhood with Eddie Seguro. Now there was blood across my knuckles. I rubbed them across my mouth. "Now what, Eddie?"

"Now you talk or I'll kill you."

"Your new business partner, Mr. Dexter Cummings, won't like to be mixed up in murder."

"I said to Mr. Cummings this morning, I said, you can't handle this guy Maguire like a high-society man. I said, let me handle him my way, the way he understands. I got to give you a hand for not lillying out on me, Maguire. You could have run, run, run. I knew you wouldn't do that; you're not that kind of a guy. But just in case, we had men staked out all over that Forrester house ever since you went back there last night. Now, why don't you be a good boy and start talking?"

"If I talk at all, Eddie, it won't be to you. Why don't you telephone Mr. Cummings? Tell him your way didn't work either. Tell him to take a cab down here and try his high-class methods again."

Seguro shook his ugly head. "It wouldn't look good. Cummings thinks I'm a big man in my business. He's got respect for me. It won't look good for me to crawl on my belly back to him."

"Cummings wants information. You haven't got a chance in the world of getting it out of me. If I make a deal at all it will be with Cummings directly. He'll respect you for producing results, Eddie. Call him up and tell him I'm ready to make a deal."

He thought for a minute. "I'm warning you, Maguire, if I get him over here and you play tricks, I'll let you have it personally, no matter what, even if I don't get a dime for doing it."

"I'm going to the bathroom, Eddie, and get cleaned up. Call Cummings and get him over here."

"You know there isn't a possible way out of here, Maguire. You won't get tricky."

"You say you're a big man, Eddie, and you still think like a punk." I walked out of there, wandered through the endless rooms until I found a bathroom. I washed up, put myself back together the best I could, even found some Band Aids in the medicine chest. In a household like Eddie's there must be lots of small accidents. I even dabbed on a little of his private stock of toilet water. If I was going out of this world, I was going smelling like a rose.

Eddie was at his desk in the library when I went back in, the gun still in hand. The room had been straightened, tables and lamps turned right side up and the debris of beat-up henchmen swept out so that everything was nice and old-English looking again. "Cummings will be right over," Seguro said.

I took a cigar from the box on the desk. I very seldom smoke cigars, but I did this to aggravate Eddie. I sat in a nice easy chair and thought about the life I had been living lately; big houses, big apartments, libraries, parlors.... the works. Being rich has its advantages. I thought about my own apartment, the narrow living room, the small bedroom, the kitchen which collapsed out of a wall. Being rich has its advantages.

Dexter Cummings arrived, dapper and unruffled. He would have been a good match for Rourke; they would have made a hell of a team. Both of them have that refined, well-bred exterior and the stuff inside to run the world with the authority of a gangster. Together they could have done anything. Then I thought maybe if they had been together, they would be happy, the edge would be off, there wouldn't be the drive to destroy each other and each other's castles.

He shook hands with me and looked over at Seguro. "What happened?"

"He wants to talk to you," Seguro grunted.

"Tell him the whole story, Eddie," I said. "Tell him how you shanghaied me here, turned your boys loose to soften me up so I would talk. Then tell him what happened to your boys, Eddie. Tell him how when I got through with them you used them for sweeping compound to clean up the floor."

Cummings cracked a smile. "Good show, eh?"

"A bloody good show," I answered. "Beats any Harvard-Yale game you ever saw. What a guy like Eddie doesn't understand is that he has to end up the way he is now, with a gun in his own hand. Eventually he's going to be backed up against his last wall with his gun drawn, and somebody's going to plug his little body full of holes."

Seguro snarled. "If it wasn't for you, Mr. Cummings, this wise guy would be a dead one. He would be very dead and his body would be ashes all the way through. Say the word and I use this gun now."

"Take it easy, Seguro. I'll talk to Maguire."

"You'll talk to me alone, Cummings. Laughing boy has got to go."

"All right, Seguro, clear out. I'll handle this."

"I think I'd better stay, Mr. Cummings. I think you're going to need me."

I broke in on their plans. "I've got a great idea, Eddie. You scram, but leave Mr. Cummings your gun. Give him your pocket handkerchief, too, Eddie, so he can hold the gun without leaving fingerprints and if he has to use it the powder burns will be on your handkerchief, not his."

"I won't need the gun," Cummings said.

Seguro gave it to him anyway, all wrapped in a pocket handkerchief like I said. He left then, grumbling like a running motor. As soon as the door closed both Cummings and I laughed. Cummings threw the handkerchief and gun on the desk where I could reach it as fast as he could. "You're ready to make a deal, Maguire?"

"I want to do some talking first. I didn't know about you and Rourke yesterday. I didn't know the history of what I was involved in."

"Very ancient history, Maguire. I'm surprised Rourke talks about it. I know she can never forget it but she has a way of blocking things out of her consciousness."

"Rourke didn't tell me. Your brother-in-law did. I was surprised. I had no way of knowing. I'm sorry, Cummings."

"You're in love with her too. I knew that yesterday. I knew it when I saw you."

"Not so fast. I honest-to-God don't know if I'm in love with her or not. You get so you don't know what love is any more."

"Not I. I always know what love is. Love is what I felt for Rourke; love is the thing we had together. I always know what love is because nothing has ever been like that again. Do you have to smoke that cigar? You smell like Seguro."

I squashed it out. "Funny that you and I should be mixed up with the same woman."

"Maybe. Why don't we both write long lovelorn letters to Ann Landers about it, get it off our chests so we can get down to the business of the moment."

"You realize your motivation in trying to get control of the Forrester Industries," I said.

"Would you like me to lie down for the full psychiatric treatment. I would never suspect you of being a parlor-game psychoanalyst, Maguire."

"Sometimes a guy is so close to something he can't recognize it for what it is."

"I suggest you listen to your own advice. I think Eddie Seguro is so close to murdering you that you can't see it or believe it. I know all about me. I know all about why I'm doing and what I'm doing. It makes no difference how aware I am of my psychological motivations. Sure, there's revenge and hurt and all the mumbo-jumbo of my subconscious mind. But, interestingly enough, gaining control of the Forrester Industries is also a very sound financial manipulation. Maybe it's incidental to the rejected-lover role you think I'm playing, but it does make a lot of sense as a business maneuver. The Forrester Industries haven't begun to tap their resources. You don't know what money is until I get hold of the Industries and begin turning the potential into dollars. Carleton Donnelly did a lot. But Carleton Donnelly was hurt and everyone hated him. He froze up, grew old. He held the Industries back by his reactionary methods, by not acknowledging labor as power and using that power. He was not intelligent enough or secure enough to develop with the times. Carleton Donnelly stopped thinking at the beginning of World War II. He spent the time since then maintaining a status quo, not giving an inch toward social advancement and not gaining ground in the development of the businesses he owned. Sure, the Forrester stock has gone up. Most stocks have. Even their dividends have increased. But not proportionately to similar businesses. The stock should be worth three times what it is today. The stockholders should be receiving dividends three to four times what they receive. When I get hold of the Industries, you watch, Maguire. You watch what happens."

"I maybe ought to buy some stock."

"If you take my deal, take the money I pay you and buy all the stock you can get. You'll treble your money in two to three years."

"I'll level with you, Cummings. I know what's in Carleton Donnelly's will. Seguro's men couldn't beat it out of me, his gun couldn't scare it out of me and you can't talk it out of me. You probably won't believe this but I like the Donnelly clan, I like Carleton Donnelly's children. I want to help them if I can. I'd like to see them come out of this happier people. Do I sound terribly corny?" He didn't answer. "I guess I do. Old Father Maguire leading his flock to green pastures. Well, corn-ball or not, it's the way I feel. There are four potentially good people there, people who have the dough to be great people. If I can help them, I want to. If telling you what the will contains would help them, I'd tell you in a minute. But I can't see how you can help them now. If I thought your getting control of the Industries would release them all to become happy people, I'd be on your side all the way."

"There's the money, Maguire. There's all that money I'm offering you."

"The money doesn't mean anything. I can get money from them. Look, I'm not trying to bargain with you. I'm not playing you against them. I'm telling you how I feel."

"You leave me no choice, Maguire. If you don't talk, I'm committed to turning you over to Eddie Seguro."

Then he saw that I was holding the gun. "Don't look surprised, Cummings. I know it isn't gamesmanship to pick up the gun after you were so sporty about leaving it openly on the desk. I know there should have been a gentleman's agreement about not picking it up. No one with an old-school tie would have taken the gun and used it against you. But you and I don't wear the same school tie. I went to school with Eddie Seguro, remember? In our crowd if a guy is sap enough to leave a gun lying around he deserves to have it used against him. I gave you your chance,

Cummings. I suggested you hold the gun, even gave you a way to cover fingerprints. I was honest with you. More than that I cannot be. Now, you walk real close to me." I moved up beside him so that he could feel the hard end of the gun. "You and I are going to leave this joint without any gunfire or fanfare. Do you mind dropping me off at the Forrester place? It isn't too far out of your way."

CHAPTER TEN

"How does the other man look?" the dragon lady asked. I touched my areas of Bauer and Black. "They both look worse," I said. "But you look great." She did. Sylvia Newman had changed into a black dress with kind of a surprise ending, a fishtail deal that attracted a grown man like pigtails do a small boy.

"Do your wounds need any licking or healing?"

"Both, and that's the best offer I've had so far today." We were in the foyer of the Forrester Mansion surrounded by throngs of people who had come to pay their last respects to Carleton Donnelly. "Where are the children?"

"Rourke is making small talk with your illustrious silver-tongued senator. I must say they make a lovely couple. When I think of how much good one well-placed bomb could do..."

"Don't be bitter. Rourke is going to be your sister, dear."

"Sister-in-law, Mr. Maguire. There's quite a difference."

"Why don't you cut this Mr. Maguire bit. Talk to me friendly. Call me something endearing."

"Like lover?" She smiled that good set of well-maintained teeth. "I've been hearing about that. Your friend Russell has been tempting me with tall tales of your aptitude."

"My aptitude? You make it sound so fancy. It's just a plain old aptitude like any other guy's on the block. Anyway, Russ has got me beat off the map. He's the real lover... body and soul. He has recommendations from all over the world, Good Housekeeping Seal of Approval, great prowess on a Posturepedic."

"I'll tell all my friends about both of you."

I gave her what I consider my sly look. "You're not having any?"

"Me?" She pointed that red dagger fingernail at herself. "Why, I'm an engaged woman, lover. I wouldn't dream...I take that back. I would dream but I wouldn't do it—" she patted my beat-up face—"so why don't you little boys give up. I'm flattered by your attentions but save your strength. I'm saving mine," she said, "for the man I love."

"I know a four-letter word."

Now she slapped my face where she had been gently patting it. "I bet you know lots of four-letter words and I bet I know just what they all mean. But save them, lover, for some other girl in some other place."

"I surrender. I give up. Now where are the children?"

"Funny, you keep calling them children. They are, really they are Carleton Donnelly's children. I don't know where they are. They've been caucusing all afternoon. Tell me, did Forrester do as well as he reported to me?"

"You're a hell of a coach, kid. He did great. He gave it that old college try. But he's got tough competition. He's up against a big man in Rourke. But young Forrester did you proud."

"Curious about the will. No one would have dreamed the estate would be divided equally."

"It makes it tough for you, doesn't it? There's nothing to contest, nothing legal to fight against. The old boy was a smart one. He precluded any unseen eventualities."

"Like me?"

"Exactly," I said. "His will, on the surface, is a document of a man who forgives and forgets. His words are benevolent words. He has made it harder for you, Sylvia. You have no one to fight now but Rourke."

"And you're on her side?"

"I'm on no one's side. I don't know enough about it yet. But keep pitching, kid. I can be had pretty easy."

"How?"

I put my hand under the fishtail back of her dress and slapped her rump very tenderly. "That's all propaganda you hear about the way to a man's heart being through his stomach."

"I wish I weren't committed to being a lady throughout this ordeal."

"What would you do?"

"I would add to your wounds, Mr. Maguire. I scratch and claw and kick and swear. I would behave like what you think I am. Then, when it was all over, I might invite you and your aptitude up to the Chinese Room."

I leaned close to her, whispered in her ear. "And I would come." Then I took off to find the children. They were nowhere on the first floor. I did manage to wave across the senator and catch Rourke's eyes. I tried the bedrooms on the second floor and they were all empty. A big staircase led to the third floor. It was too important architecturally to be servants' stairs so I decided to explore. At the far end of the dark third-floor corridor was a burst of bright light blazing through two glass doors. This was a children's playroom and it wasn't like any other room in the house. This was a happy room, warmed by sunlight, a room to laugh in and sing in. Russell and Forrester were there, sitting at a low table in children's chairs made of scrolled wicker. Neither of them heard me as I came in. They were both bent over the table in deep concern. What was concerning them was a checker game.

"Who's winning?"

Russ didn't look up. It was his move. Forrester said, "Pull up a chair, Johnny. You can play the winner."

"Is this all you have to do? There must be five hundred people wearing out the carpet downstairs. You know what Rourke is going to say. She's going to start bellyaching again that you always run off and leave her with all the burdens."

"Sonny, you have me beat again," Russ said, shoving the game aside. "He always did beat me at checkers."

"And Parcheesi and Monopoly." His younger brother smiled.

Russell said, "Say, that used to be a hell of a game. Monopoly. The four of us used to play it all the time."

"I bet Rourke won," I said.

They both laughed and at the same moment stopped laughing. "She used to buy up all the little property," Russ explained. "I always wanted to own the Boardwalk and Park Place, the expensive stuff, but Rourke used to buy up all the cheap property and build hotels. You're right, Maguire, she beat us every time."

"But not this time," Forrester said. "This time we're playing for keeps."

"You and Russ have formed a coalition?"

Forrester nodded, looking over to Russ for confirmation.

Russ stood up and walked to the window. "I'm not used to thinking," he said. "I'm not used to figuring things out. I've lived my life from hour to hour. I've lived it with my heart open and my pants down. I've never had to think about anything. People have taken care of me; they've wanted to. It's a wasted life, I know that; and when this is over, I'll go back to wasting it, and I know that too. I can't change any more. I'm supposed to go to Hollywood to make a picture. I'll make the picture and then I'll drift off again. That's my pattern. I don't fight it anymore." He turned to us. "But just this once I have the power to do something good, something helpful. I have to use my brain, think it out. I'm going along with Forrester for a couple of reasons. First of all, this is his. Everything by rights belongs to Forrester. He is the Forrester heir, not Rourke and not me. We're intruders here, we always were. He's the Forrester and he has his rights.

"But that isn't the big thing," Russell went on. "The big thing is life and being able to live it. This is Sonny's chance to blossom out, step forward and take what belongs to him, use this wealth and this power to do something decent and good. If I can help him find himself, be what he wants to be, then I'll do it."

Forrester smiled at his brother, gave him a look of love. "You've always helped me, Russ. You've always taken my side."

"It isn't that simple, Sonny. It isn't taking your side against Rourke. I don't want to hurt your feelings, kid, but you must know that the ties between Rourke and me are the strongest ties. It isn't that I like her better or think she's a better person. It has to do with blood and vague dreams I had when I was a kid. Rourke is me, in a way. Rourke is what I could have been. Let's face it, Rourke is a man. She thinks like a man, acts like a man. She's beautiful and she screws like a woman but that's as far as it goes. Basically, she's a man. She's the man I should be. She's the man her father was. Everything got so fouled up. Rourke turned out to be a man and I rattle around the country like a whore, people taking care of me, people supporting me for what kicks they can get out of it."

"You're being hard on yourself, Russ," Forrester said.

"No, I'm not, Sonny. I'm not complaining. Leading a whore's life has its advantages. At least I'm a good whore. Everyone likes me. I go to parties, I travel all over the world. Only good things happen to me. I'm not complaining. What I'm trying to say is that now I have a chance to turn this thing around, change the spots on the leopard. I forced Rourke to be a man and now I have the power to turn her back into a woman by forcing her out of the Industries. You helped me make up my mind about that, Maguire. You're good for Rourke. This won't be a defeat for her. She'll lose the Industries but she'll wind up with you. I think she loves you, Maguire. I never remember her loving anyone except Dex. When she lost him I never thought she'd love again. But she loves you, Maguire. She'll be free to love you if she isn't saddled with the Industries."

"You're taking a lot for granted, Russ. I never said I loved Rourke, and Rourke never said she loved me."

"Don't tell me about love, Maguire. I can see it better than you. Look at you, battered and bruised. What for? Legal duty? Hell, no. You're in love. I envy you."

"He's right, Johnny. Russ is always right about love."

Young Forrester offered his hand for me to shake. I put my arm around his shoulder instead. "You guys are just anxious for a brother-in-law. I'm an innocent bystander here. Don't count me in on your thinking."

"All my life, no matter where I was," Russ said, "Rourke, Sonny and Mary have been on my conscience. No matter where I am, I worry about them, about their happiness. Don't you see, Maguire, this is the chance for all of them? Even Mary. She's got that Randy Lawrence chasing her. It's no secret what he's after. His old man and Dex have put him up to it, sure. But there have been slimmer bases for marriage. He'll make Mary happy. You can fix it, Maguire, so he'll always have to make her happy. You set up her inheritance so that he can't touch it without her. That way he'll always have to stay chasing her. There have been other marriages like that and they've worked out fine." He slapped his hands together. "This is my chance to right all the wrongs, turn everything right side up."

"Except for yourself, Russ." I sat in one of the small chairs and built blocks with the checkers. "You have everyone taken care of but yourself."

Russ shook his head, smiling into the sunlight. "All I ask is that they be happy. I'm a different breed of cat. There's no salvation for me. I don't want any."

Mary came in then, laughing and tossing her head like a heated mare. Randy Lawrence followed her, his face flushed. "We've been going through all those horrible old photograph albums. They are so funny. Rand recognized all those girls you had your picture taken with, Russ. Those pictures are so funny." She noticed me then. "What happened? How did you hurt yourself?"

"Small accident, Mary. Nothing serious."

She put her arms around me. "We are giving you a bad time, aren't we? I'm sorry, Johnny. You are a love and we love you." Her body stiffened as she felt the hard steel of Eddie Seguro's gun in my pocket. She reached in, drew it out and held it at arm's length as though it were a dead rat.

I took the gun away from her and put it back into my pocket. I held my hand out to Randy Lawrence. "The Donnelly children have bad manners. My name is John Maguire."

I could tell by the look on his face as we shook hands that there had been some hanky-panky going along with the looking at old pictures. He was no kid, this Randy Lawrence. He had a clean-cut look, honest eyes and a firm handshake. Russ was probably right. There were many marriages based on slimmer grounds. These people had background in common, and money. How many people did I know whose marriage was founded on nothing firmer than a careless moment at a picnic. Russ was probably right.

"Mary has told me about you, John. I am as glad as she is that you have come here to help them." He took Mary's hand and smiled at her. "It's pretty disrespectful to be laughing the way we are but ... well, Mary and I have known each other a long time, but just to say hello to. But today, in a couple of hours, we've caught up for a lot of lost years."

"I'm not ashamed to laugh," Mary said. "No one could laugh in this house while he was alive. I think it's absolutely marvelous that we can all laugh and be gay now. We're going to be so happy ... all of us. Even Rourke. We have you to thank for that, Johnny."

I laughed at her. "You know I used to think there was nothing worse than Irish women who got together and arranged marriages over the back fence or across the porch. My own mother was like that, matchmaking with her friends. But those women were amateurs compared to you people. Real amateurs."

Forrester said. "I'd better find Sylvia. She'll be wondering about me."

"Sylvia's all right. I saw her downstairs."

Mary said, "Why don't you go down and get her, Sonny? Why don't we all stay up here and laugh and laugh and laugh. It's so wonderful to laugh. It's so wonderful to have something to laugh about."

"You'll all like Sylvia when you get to know her," Forrester said. "On the surface she doesn't seem like our kind of people. Her background is different from ours. She's been poor and we've never been poor. She's hard to know at first. It took me time. I had never met anyone like her before. She was cum laude at NYU. She's really bright as hell. You may think she wears too much make-up or dresses extreme, but she'll get used to us, get used to our ways."

Mary was blinded with love. "She's lovely, Sonny, she's just lovely. She'll be perfect for you. She's what we all need to keep us on our toes. Can you imagine a cum laude in our family? We're all so damn stupid. I mean you always had to work so hard at school, Sonny." She looked at Russ. "You probably could have been cum laude if you'd ever stayed at a school long enough."

"Give Sylvia a chance," Forrester said. "All she needs is a little confidence." Russ turned, his mouth opened to say something. He changed his mind. "Do you think it would be all right if we took this third floor and converted it into an apartment? It's just about my share of the house if you count the basement and the servants' quarters. I've always liked it up here. The happiest times we had were always up here with Mother. Remember when she used to play that piano for us?" He looked quickly around the room. "Hey, what happened to the piano?"

"It's right in there," Mary said, "in the storeroom. It's loaded with dust. Let's move it in, shall we? Come on, we have four strong men. Let's move it in."

The other three started to follow Mary. "I think you ought to wait," I said. "After all, there's ... well. I think you ought to wait."

Russ pushed me along. "You're getting just like Rourke, Maguire. Snap out of it. Come on, we need your strong back."

The piano was sadly out of tune and Mary played very badly. They found an old song book, sang, laughed and exchanged reminiscences of their childhood. I retreated to a corner, straddled an old hobby horse which creaked and splintered under my weight. Randy Lawrence came over to talk to me.

"If you knew them better, you wouldn't disapprove," he said. "This hasn't been a house of laughing and singing since Dolly Forrester died."

"It just seems odd with their father in an open coffin downstairs."

"It will be better for all of them now. For everyone."

I was looking to find something I didn't like about Lawrence. But he didn't appear to be any more than what the surface showed, a nice-mannered well-bred man, slightly gray at the temples and taken in by the drama he was forced to act in. "What do you do for a living, Lawrence?"

He smiled easily. "Is this an official interrogation?"

"I'm very fond of Mary," I said.

"You have it all figured out, don't you? My father told me what you and Rourke think. You think that Father and Dexter have put me up to this." He shook his head. "I suppose in the background somewhere I know that they would like to see me marry into the family. It would benefit them; it would be good for me, too. I work for Hiawatha Paper Mills, a division of the Forrester Industries."

"That figures."

"Listen, Maguire, all I'm doing is showing Mary a little attention, something she's never had. You're way ahead of me. I've only known the girl since yesterday really. Yesterday and today. Right away you have a federal case against me."

"How old are you, Lawrence?"

"Twenty-eight. Old enough. You want the complete history?" I didn't say anything. It was his ball, I was letting him carry it. "I'm the only son of an ambitious mother and a frightened father.

Except for the Army, I've never lived away from home. I've sowed my wild oats and I don't have any venereal disease. I'm not the brightest guy in the world and it doesn't bother me. What other information do you have to give Rourke about me?"

"Like I said, Lawrence, I'm fond of Mary. She's had a rough time. She's out of the cocoon. She's a butterfly, and you know how butterflies are. They get out in the sun and the light dazzles them. They can get into trouble. They can bang against a windowpane and get hurt. I don't want to see Mary hurt. I want her to come out of this cocoon slowly, take her time about finding out who she is and what living is all about."

"She needs someone to look after her. I know that. Maybe I'm the guy to do it and maybe I'm not. Hell, I'm not saying I'm going to marry the girl. You're jumping the gun. We're still at the getting-acquainted stage."

"Let me see your handkerchief?"

"My handkerchief? What for?"

"Let me see it." I took it from his pocket. It was stained with lipstick.

He took it back from me, arranged it carefully and put it in his breast pocket. "So what?"

"So she's just out of the cocoon and she's itchy. I know that. I'm asking you to understand about Mary. Don't let her rush into anything."

"Are you telling me or threatening me?"

I thought about that for a moment. "I'm threatening you, Lawrence. I don't care how bad she wants it, lay off. It's for her own good. I know what I'm talking about."

"You ought to get together with Russ. He's had a heart-to-heart talk with me. You and Russ don't see eye to eye."

"Russ is a damn fool."

"Yes, I suppose he is. But I wish I was like him. I wish I had the guts to live the way he lives. I wish I was like Russ. Beats me why the old man included him in the will."

The jerks, I was thinking. The stupid, stupid jerks. "So you got that out of her, huh. You got her to tell you what was in the will."

"The information was volunteered. They had a business meeting, the three of them, and Mary insisted I listen in."

"Well, what are you waiting for? Why aren't you on the telephone to your Uncle Dexter. He's dying to hear the news."

Lawrence sat on the floor and crossed his legs as if he was going to play jacks. "I told you I wasn't the brightest guy in the world, Maguire. But I'm also not the dumbest. I know how bad Dexter wants that information."

"So you're going in business for yourself. I'll say you're not the dumbest. Let me give you a tip, Lawrence—hold out for big money. They play rough, those boys. Look at me. It just happens I play rougher. I don't think you can. Ask a big price and give your uncle the information like a good little boy."

"I have a secret to tell you, Maguire. I don't like Uncle Dexter. All my life, I've had Uncle Dexter as a shining example to me. My mother's dear little brother. Uncle Dexter did this when he was your age and Uncle Dexter never did that. Uncle Dexter graduated with honors. Uncle Dexter never took out waitresses. Uncle Dexter knew an opportunity when he saw it. Maybe if I weren't related to Uncle Dexter I would like him. But this way I'm a failure because Uncle Dexter is a success. Until now." He looked up from the floor. "Am I getting through to you, Maguire?"

"Keep talking."

He studied the floor again, making doodles with his fingers in the thin dust. "Maybe soon I can say Uncle Dexter never got a piece of the Forrester Industries, but I did." He laughed. "Can you imagine the expression on my parent's faces? And Dexter's? Wow!"

"What are you going to be when you grow up, Lawrence?"

"You tell me, Maguire. I'm open for offers. The way I see it, I'm in a pretty good bargaining position. I tell you leave me alone and you have to. If you don't, I call Uncle Dexter and make a deal with him."

"And if I leave you alone?"

"I don't know. I have to think about what I want. I know what I don't want. I don't want to be Chairman of the Board. I don't even want my father to be Chairman of the Board. I think it's a fine idea if Forrester is. I want a boat. Did you ever want a boat, Maguire? I don't want a very big boat, nothing oceangoing, but I like the water. I want a nice house in Lake Forest. It's close to the country club; most of my married friends live around there. And I like to hunt. I've always wanted to raise and train my own hunting dogs. And something else, I've never been to Europe. There's a whole string of golf courses through Scotland I'd like to try. I'm a pretty fair golfer. Do you play?"

"Anyone for tennis?"

He laughed. "I guess I do know what I want. I want what most guys break their backs working to get and then are so damn worn out they can't enjoy them. I can get these things very easily. All I do is keep my mouth shut, fall in love with Mary, play ball with Forrester. And you can't spoil that for me. You don't dare tell Mary. First of all she wouldn't believe you. And if you did, I'd make a deal with Uncle Dexter and you would have gotten beat up for nothing. Your hands are tied, aren't they Maguire?"

The children had found some old costumes in a trunk. Each one wore a funny hat and the boys held wooden swords painted silver. They were singing something from Gilbert and Sullivan. They were in another world.

"Admit it, Maguire. Your hands are tied. Talk it over with Rourke. I'm sure she'd rather see Mary married to me than to see Dex get control of the Industries."

"I've been thinking about your Uncle Dexter. He hired a gangster to work me over. I could do the same with you, only I wouldn't have to hire anyone. I can be a gangster all by myself. I have a gun in my pocket; you saw that. I used it on your Uncle

Dexter not more than an hour ago. It got me out of a tight spot. I can use it on you."

He knew I was bluffing. "Look, Maguire, everything doesn't always have to be either black or white. Things can be good and bad at the same time. I'm not a bad guy, I'm not doing anything to hurt anyone. I'll make Mary happy. I'll teach her to like the things I like, nice things. We'll have kids and a house. We'll go to Europe on our honeymoon. All the things that she thought would never happen, will happen. I can make them happen. It's a good deal for both of us."

The way he said it, it made sense. It was what Russ had said. It was even what Mary had predicted for herself. This associating with rich people was raising hell with my sense of values. I didn't even feel like slugging Randy Lawrence any more. He was a personable guy and he was making what sounded like a sensible deal for himself and for Mary. Things like this didn't happen in my old neighborhood. Middle-class moral standards are higher there. If a man pulls something like this, he doesn't admit it to anyone, not even to himself. This was so polite, so easily said. And damned if I wasn't beginning to think it was a good idea.

I was aware then that the music had stopped, the singing had stopped. There was an ominous silence. There was Rourke at the door, biting her lip to keep from crying. She looked from one to the other, hating us all. She ran to the piano, slammed the keyboard closed, narrowly missed catching Mary's finger in the impact of the slam. She tried to speak, but when she opened her mouth only a shriek came out and she started to cry, hard tears from deep inside. She ran from the room, not able to control herself.

We all knew what she was feeling, the depth of her grief, the extent of her hurt. They felt it and I felt it. We were stunned speechless by it. We were little people and she was a big person, capable of big emotion. I was more at fault than anyone. These were children playing children's games and not knowing more than children know. With their wooden swords and play-acting hats, they were grotesque marionettes, their faces painted stupid, never to change expression. I hated them now, I hated them with Rourke's hatred. And I hated myself for being taken in by them, caught in their hollow make-believe.

"Rourke!" I called her name and ran after her down the stairs. She ran into a room and slammed the door. I rammed it just as she was turning the lock. The impact forced the door open, caught Rourke off balance and threw her to the floor. She lay there sobbing. I kicked the door shut, locked it, lay beside her on the floor, my face rubbing against her hair. "Don't cry, Rourke. Please, don't cry. Come on, stop it now." She pushed me away with the spikes of her fingernails, stood up, ran to the bed and flung herself on it, still crying. "Red, they didn't mean anything. They're stupid. They have no feeling. Me, too, Red. I'm stupid, too. I should have stopped them. Don't cry. Please." She fought me savagely, clawing at me, hitting me, tearing my shirt. I held still for her, let myself be the target for her anger. The wounds on my face opened up and I felt the blood begin again and I saw my blood on her hands. Yet I lay still, took the punishment. I felt no physical pain. What I was feeling for her was greater than that.

When she stopped, broke away, tried to leave the bed, I grabbed at her, caught her dress. It ripped as she fought to be free of me. Her body was an animal's body, with that kind of power. She tore free of the dress, ran half-naked across the room and into the closet. I followed her inside. She was hiding herself in the jungle of clothes. I grabbed her arm, tried to pull her out. She bit my arm, caught me off guard, attacked me again with the strength of a wildcat. In the struggle we both fell to the floor pulling clothes on top of us. We were a snake pit of hissing bodies clawing at each other, snarled by the clothes. In a lightning move, she slipped out of my grasp. I lay for a moment on the floor breathing heavy, bleeding hard. My suitcoat was ripped half off. I got out of it, left it on the floor and went back into the room after her.

She was poised at the far end of the room. She was naked from the waist up, her breasts pointed high as she held her hands over her head. One hand clutched a heavy bronze bookend. I was too dazed to see it clearly. I moved toward her and she flung it at me. It caught me in the shoulder and I reeled back against the wall. I started for her again. She started throwing books; they came one after the other, some hit me and some missed. It didn't matter. I kept walking toward her until she was trapped between me and the wall. I stopped. She dared me with her eyes to come any closer. I stood still, waiting for her to move. She feinted one way and then lunged past me on the other side. I clutched at her, tripped, fell to the floor and my hands were full of the soft silk of her slip still warm from her body.

I looked up at the naked beauty of her. "Rourke," I said. My voice came out a whisper. My head fell down and I lay dead for a minute. Rourke's tears had changed to laughter; she was laughing at me. I raised up, wiped my face with the soft, blue silk, staining it bright red with blood, making it wet with sweat.

When I was on my feet I loosened my tie and pulled it off, started toward her again. She was still laughing, louder now. I was in front of her and the sound of the laughter was deafening. I cracked her across the face with my open hand. She stopped, bewildered for a minute. Then her claws reached out for me again, ripped at my shirt, pulled it off my body with the zigzag screech of ripping cloth. I pushed her away and for a moment my hands tingled with the touch of her flesh. I took off my belt, wrapped the end of it around my hand, and held it as a whip. She came at me again but my arm wouldn't come down to strike her. Her teeth sank into my arm, my hand opened and the belt dropped like a dead snake. She kept her bite as she worked swiftly with her hands until I was as naked as she.

I grabbed her hair, pulled her head back until she let loose of me. I pushed away, hard. She fell to the floor, partly against the wall, drawn up in a circle like a wounded cat. I put my arm to my mouth, sucked in the blood of the wound her teeth had made.

She crawled to me. She crawled on the floor until her face was at my feet. Her hands went up to touch my legs and where there had been claws and clawing there was now tenderness, a touch of love. With my mouth I sucked harder at the wound. My eyes closed when I felt the soft wetness of her lips against one leg and then the other, the pattern of her kisses following the trail of her hands up my body. Then the splash of her hair against my skin as her face turned from one leg to the other. Her hands stopped at my waist, her arms went around me and she clung to me, hung from me. It was more than I could stand and yet I stood it, stood rigid and erect, afraid to move. The soft, wet touch of her mouth continued. I felt my own teeth sink into my arm, over the marks of her teeth. I was fighting back the flood of feeling in my own body, saving it to build up to the dizzy heights of its own power. I bit harder to hold it back. Then it was no use; it was more power than anyone could control. I opened my mouth and my arm fell to my side. For more than a second I enjoyed the ecstasy of holding back. Then I took her, drew her straight up against me, picked her up, carried her in my arms to the closet and we sank together to the bed of tangled clothes.

CHAPTER ELEVEN

"Cut that out, Maguire," she said. I was steeping in a hot bathtub, Rourke was dressing my wounds, leaning over me so that one breast brushed my face. "Stop doing that or I'll hurt you."

"Ouch."

"Now what?"

"It hurts. Take it easy on that iodine; it burns."

"Don't be a sissy."

"My arm looks as if it spent that afternoon with a couple of tigers."

"Just one tiger," she said. "Now, get out of that bathtub so I can patch the rest of you." She shook her head. "What a mess."

"I had a rough afternoon. Hand me a towel." I stepped out of the tub. I used the towel with very little pressure. I really was beat up, happy but beat. As soon as I got an area dried off, Rourke went to work with the iodine and bandages.

"How did you get this one back here?" she asked. "This must be from some other soiree, but to show you that I'm a good sport, I'll bandage it anyway."

"Something just occurred to me."

"What?"

"How am I going to get back to my own room without clothes? If I tried to put my other clothes back on the butler will arrest me midway in the hall as a vagrant. Ouch. Watch what you're doing."

"Sorry. It's very simple. I'll get the clothes out of your room and you can dress in here. One more spot and you'll be as good as new."

I looked myself over. "You see this?" I pointed to a large bandaged area on my hip. "No one hit me there. You just gave first aid to a birthmark."

She ripped off the adhesive. "How was I to know? It doesn't look like a birthmark." She patted the last bandage in place. "There. As good as new. You're all ready to go out again to battle."

"Why don't you get dressed so that you can get my clothes? It must be close to dinner time."

"You go in there and wait. I'll be right in."

The bed was soft. I could have fallen asleep and slept through to the next day. I guess I had begun to doze when Rourke came back into the room and began to dress.

"You know we're in trouble, don't you?"

"It's a constant state with me," Rourke said.

"They've told Randy Lawrence what's in the will."

"They didn't! I don't believe it. I know they're stupid but ... well, they're not disloyal. I don't believe it."

"Straight from Mr. Lawrence's mouth I got it. The children have taken him into their confidence.

"This is just what Dexter needs. This is just the ammunition he needs. I don't know what he'll do but he'll do everything to keep us fighting with each other until the five days are up. Holy cow, Maguire, how could they? They're so damned stupid. Mary I can understand, but Russ would know better. Forrester, too. It's a wonder he didn't see the danger for himself. Dex wouldn't want young Forrester either. That's just great. What do I do now, send my head to Dex on a silver platter?"

"It's not as hopeless as it seems. Young Lawrence has decided to play it fancy, double-cross his Uncle Dexter. Lawrence thinks he has more to gain by stringing along with Mary, playing ball with Forrester. He confessed that he didn't like his Uncle Dexter, wouldn't mind seeing Uncle Dexter out and himself in."

"Everybody wants to be head of the Forrester Industries."

"You have it wrong. Lawrence doesn't want that. He wants Mary and a boat and a house and a trip to Europe and to live happily ever after."

"I knew this would happen. I knew someone would make a pass at Mary and she'd fall. My Father knew it. It was the thing he always tried to protect us from. He's gone one day, and bang! it happens. Poor Mary. It hurts so much when you find out the truth. When the horrible realization comes it hurts like hell."

"Lawrence has given me an ultimatum. Leave him alone to work things out with Mary in his way or he runs to tell Uncle Dexter the news. I don't think it's a bad idea to play along with Lawrence."

"I think it's a stinking idea. I wouldn't give him the satisfaction. Throw him out, Maguire. Let him run to Uncle Dexter. I'll handle it. I've handled Dex before and I can do it again." She had put on another black dress. She was leaning close to a mirror, applying lipstick.

"It isn't as simple as that. The forces against you seem to be formidable at the moment. Russ has joined up with young Forrester, and where Russ goes Mary goes. I assume this is old family history. And giving them moral support from the sidelines are the dragon lady and Randy Lawrence."

"All to be expected. I'll fight them alone. I always have."

"You're not alone, Red."

She came over to the bed, sat next to me, touched me. "Thank you, Maguire. I like knowing I have moral support."

I grabbed her, pulled her down on top of me. "Want to make it immoral support?"

"Some other time." She bit my ear and drew away.

"The way I figure it, Red, they have a better chance of winning than you. You see, they don't feel about Dexter Cummings the way you do. If there isn't unanimity among you, the worst that can happen for them is that they all wind up with a lot of ready cash rather than their shares in the Industries. I have a sneaking suspicion that Sylvia and Randy are going to advise this. Even if they asked me what to do, I'll tell them to out bluff you. The weakness in your case, Red, is that you'd rather see young Forrester take over than to let go of your holdings, let them fall in Cummings's hands. If they stick to their guns, you'll relent at the last minute, hand it over to Forrester and then go to work to run him the way you ran your father. Next best to being the big man yourself is to be the man behind the man. If they'd ask me, I would have to tell them that. I hope to God they don't ask me. Sylvia Newman is bright; she'll arrive at this conclusion all by herself." I sat up. "Tell me the truth, Red. What would you do if they held out, if they would rather see the stock sold than have you take over? What would you do?"

"That's not the point, Maguire. The thing to be thinking about is how to avoid reaching that point. What could happen to split them, break up the coalition. I have to think of something to dynamite their combine. They all have too much damn self-confidence at the moment. Forrester has the dragon lady and Mary has Randy and Russ has being on the wagon."

"You have me, Red."

"Do I?"

"Yep. Battered body and soul, I'm on your side now."

"That may be it, Maguire." She snapped her fingers. "That may be it. Will you marry me?"

"This is so sudden."

"Don't be funny. This is serious." She paced quickly now, forming her plan. "Well, answer my question."

I smiled at her. She really was quite a girl. "I don't think a girl should propose to a man when he's stark naked on her bed."

"Sex has nothing to do with this. I'm offering you a straight business deal."

"Not on your life. No sex, no deal."

"Can't you be serious for a minute? Don't you see how well this would work out? Think about it, Maguire. The children couldn't object. You could be head of the Forrester Industries."

"Why not? Everyone wants to be head of the Forrester Industries." Then I shook my head. "Thanks, no, Red. I'm not the type."

"But it's perfect. We tell the children that we have been secretly engaged..."

"Let's not tell them what we've been engaged in."

"We'll tell them we were planning to be married but, of course, in view of Father's death we've had to postpone our plans. It's very logical. You can head the Industries, represent all of us. They'll trust you to be fair and square. I'm sure you will be. You'll do something of what Forrester wants and you'll do something of what I want. You may even incorporate some of Sylvia Newman's ideas. It may be that you will eventually develop ideas of your own."

"Thanks a lot."

"It's a natural, Maguire. It's a perfect compromise between Forrester and me. Even if Forrester resists, Mary will go along and certainly Russ will. They can make Forrester agree. We'll all have to compromise." She stopped at the dresser, gave her hair a few fast brushes as she spoke. "The presidents of subsidiaries will play ball with that, too. They like you, Maguire. After lunch several of them commented that you reminded them of Father." She dropped the brush. "What do you say, is it a deal?"

"Slow down, Red. Slow way down." I pulled off the bedspread, wrapped myself in it. This was no discussion for being undressed in. I stood up, figuring I'd think better on my feet. "That kind of setup would be no good for us, Red."

Her voice was soft, her eyes lowered. "You said you loved me, Maguire."

I tried to remember when I had said it. It sounds dumb, but it's one thing I don't say easily. There have been lots of girls lots of times in my life and it would have been easy to tell them I loved them, string them along that way. But those words aren't easy for me to say. I said it once and had meant it. Tragedy had struck, and that love never came to life again. I never said the words after that; I was never sure. Maybe I loved Rourke, maybe I was scared to admit it to myself, afraid of being hurt, winding up zero again with hollowness haunting me. When had I said it? I couldn't remember. If I had told her I loved her it came from an unconscious source; maybe that was the real source of love, a hidden thing which is not regulated by thinking or planning. We never talked about love.

"What's the matter, Maguire, did I catch you in a line? Is that what you tell all the girls in the heat of passion?"

I shook my head. "I'm an easy man in the hay, Red; I wouldn't fool you about that. But I don't love easy—fall in love. Each man builds up a standard inside himself. The thing with me is not saying 'I love you' every time I kiss a woman. It's part of an honesty psychosis of mine. When you're poor and you don't have possessions, you can have honesty for free and it becomes a big thing. Since I was a kid and envied other kids their bicycles and wagons, I always said to myself, 'You're honest, Maguire.' And not saying 'I love you' is part of that honesty. Girls slide into the sack easier when you butter them up with talk about love. I've never done that. I said it once and meant it; it was a long time ago and everything about it is dead now and the hell with it. If I said it again, if I said it to you, I must mean it."

"You don't remember saying it? Do you think I'm lying to you, trying to trick you? Remember who I am, Maguire. Remember that I'm Rourke Donnelly and I don't need any man, I don't need any man's love, I don't have to cheat and connive to get a man to be in love with me."

"Simmer down, Red. This is important to me."

"Skip it, Maguire. It was a lousy idea. I'll go get you some clothes."

"Wait a minute." It couldn't be over that easy. "What did you say? What did you answer me? Did you say you loved me too?"

"Forget it. I'm sorry I started it." She started to leave but I held her back.

"It *is* started, Red. It's started and there's no point to stopping until it's over." I looked at her hard, tried to see beneath the surface, establish some connection with what she was feeling. "Okay, so I love you. I didn't love you yesterday. Maybe I didn't love you this morning, but I love you now."

"Don't be gallant."

"I said I loved you. What the hell do you want me to do, get down on my knees and sing 'I Love You Truly'? It's like pulling teeth to say it but I said it and I meant it. What does it mean?"

"It means that my plan will work, Maguire. Can't you see how this simplifies everything? We'll be married and you'll take over. You'll probably be the best thing that ever hit the Industries." Her voice came alive again, her eyes glowed, everything fired up again with her plot.

"When two people get married, they love each other and they live happily ever after."

"That's the story-book stuff, Maguire. Just a few minutes ago you were saying that Mary and Randy Lawrence would make a good marriage. That isn't love."

"Okay, so I'm plenty mixed up. I still think Mary and Randy are a good idea. But this is rich people's thinking, Rourke. Ever since I started up the front walk of this house I kept telling myself I was outclassed here. That includes being in love. Like I said, the girl answers the man. She says 'I love you.'"

"What do you think I am? For all the time we've known each other, what do you think I am? You want true-confession time, Maguire? All right, I'll give you a true confession. I'm not what you think I am. I don't, as you put it so quaintly, slide into the sack so easy. You have a right to think the way you do based on past performance. But that night on the lake when you fished me out of the water, I was frightened, as frightened as I can ever remember being. My defenses were down. I wanted you, I wanted you to make love to me and I wanted to love you back. It was a combination of being so close to dying, and the way the night was, the storm, the thunder and the lightning. It was you, the way you were, a strong and silent stranger to me. If there hadn't been that night, if everything had not been right for it, I would still be the virgin queen of the Forrester Mansion."

I started to say something, decided against it. But it was no good, she knew what I was thinking.

"There had been one other man, Maguire. I was nineteen years old and I thought I loved him. I thought he loved me. It didn't work out that way. The years between him and you were frozen years. And the nights between the nights I was with you were frozen nights." She sat down. "Because I can match your fervor doesn't mean I'm like you, Maguire. I don't have a man's attitude about sex. I was reared straight-laced and that doesn't rub off easily. I couldn't have done what I did with you without—well, without some feeling involved."

"Are you saying, 'I love you'?"

She shook her head. "I can't say it, Maguire. The words don't come out."

"Do you feel it?"

"I can't feel anything now. I can't allow myself to feel anything now. There's too much at stake. There are too many decisions to make, too many other things to think about. Do you realize what is involved in planning just the funeral? Do you have any idea of how many people are going to be at that church tomorrow, important people who have to be satisfied by seating protocol. And the arrangements for the procession to the cemetery, legal parade permits, the motorcycle escorts, the special cars for the governor and the mayor. I have a thousand things on my mind, important details. Besides all that I have Dexter Cummings breathing down my neck, the Board of Control hanging around here like expectant fathers. Mary and that silly Randy Lawrence. Forrester and that dreadful woman. Everything all at once, everything piling up. How can you ask me to think about love, to know what I really feel. I have to think about my responsibility. My first obligation is to that responsibility. I can't think about love. There's no time for it now."

"You put your finger on it, Red. There's no time for it. And with you and me there would never be time for it. Maybe if I *didn't* love you I'd marry you. It would be a business deal and I could make the decision on a business basis. I assume that I would have latitude in this marriage. If I kept a girl on the side and was discreet about it, you'd say go right ahead. I'd be kept in a style to which I could easily adjust myself. I might even take up golf, play with Randy Lawrence. I could buy a boat, too. We could race, me and my brother-in-law. I'd learn to dress better, more dignified, so that I'd look great at the Board of Control meeting. I'd be a nice figure for you to work behind. It's a good deal, Red. It's even a better deal than Mary is offering Randy Lawrence. He won't have the latitude I have because Mary loves him, would be jealous if he had an affair. But not you. You'll slap me on the back and pack my pajamas for me. It sounds great. It *is* great, and maybe I could do it if I wasn't in love with you. But I am in love with you. Damn it. It can come to no good. I'll only get my ass in a sling again. Funny, but now that I've said it, I want to keep saying it. It feels good to say it and it hurts to say it. All at once, it's wonderful and it's terrible. I love you, Red. That's all there is to it. I love you."

Rourke would not look at me. She bit her lip, fighting back either words or tears, I wasn't sure which. "I'll get your clothes," she said, and this time I let her go.

CHAPTER TWELVE

T HAT NIGHT the Forrester Mansion was filled again with people lined up first to view the body and to file past the children and mutter the words of condolence. Randy Lawrence was very much in evidence, talking to people, bringing Mary glasses of water, squeezing her hand or patting her head. Several times he and his father huddled in a quiet corner for a conference. I noticed that Mathew Lawrence did most of the frantic talking. His son nodded or shook his head, kept a slow smile on his face. He was enjoying this beginning of his victory. Sylvia Newman had disappeared after dinner and I was just as glad. I envied Randy Lawrence. I would have liked to bring Rourke water and whisper words to her but she wasn't that kind of woman.

The only other person who looked as lost as I did was a Catholic priest. He stood in the center of the reception hall, looking around, wanting desperately to talk to someone. I was his boy.

"Good evening, Father. It's good you came. We've had a dearth of the clergy around here. My name is John Maguire. I'm a friend of the family."

"I'm Father Kelly. Christened John, too."

"I'm a John Patrick Aloysius."

He smiled. "So am I."

"Now that we have our lodge straight, what's new? Were you a friend of Mr. Donnelly?"

"Not Carleton Donnelly. I thought I was a friend of Russell Donnelly. It's very strange, but when I went through the line before, I shook hands with him and he was very nice but I don't think he remembered me."

"Don't feel bad, Father. Russ kicks around a lot of places, meets many people. He's not always as sober as he is now. This place is so jammed with people he probably doesn't recognize anyone." Just then two men walked by to stand in line to go in the parlor. They looked familiar to me. Then I remembered who one of them was. He was the man who sat guard in Eddie Seguro's dummy apartment, the man who watched television. I cased as far as I could see, looking for other things. Seguro was up to something. I didn't know what.

"I have an orphanage," Father Kelly said. "It's how I met Russell. If you're an old friend of the family, I don't suppose this will be telling tales out of school. As a matter of fact, it shows how rich the heart can be, no matter what the body or the spirit. There's a little chapel connected with the orphanage. It's open to the street for those who wish to pray there. Very late one night I was in the chapel and I found Russell there, unconscious, smelling very badly of liquor. I got one of the other priests and we took him into the orphanage, to the infirmary. He was more than drunk, Mr. Maguire, he was very sick. Our doctor said he was malnourished and very close to pneumonia."

Any one of the men could be Seguro's man. I thought maybe I ought to alert the police, but that would get into the newspapers. I could do nothing until they started something. I could only stay on guard. Maybe they were just getting the layout, planning future action. Maybe they were going to hijack me again or try putting a bullet through my head. There was enough confusion around so that it was not an unlikely place for assassination. So many people were milling together it would be difficult to figure who fired the shot. Well, there was nothing I could do at the moment but listen to the rest of Father Kelly's story.

"Our facilities at the orphanage are limited, our space modest. But he was too sick to move and we were afraid that if we turned him over to the police he might not get the attention he needed. So we kept him at the orphanage. For a long time he was barely conscious, he didn't know where he was. I remember his bed was between a case of measles and a case of mumps. We kept his bed screened off and were very antiseptic. We don't have a contagious ward. When he began to be better we found him to be a pleasant man and the boys liked him. He liked the boys. When he was able to move around, he helped us out, read to the sick ones, played games with those on the mend. He found out that what we wanted most was a place where we could take the boys for a week or two in the summer, a place where they could swim and play ball and run free. He made some mysterious arrangements at a friend's house in Lake Forest, a big estate. He explained that people were going away for a while and they were happy to turn the place over to the boys. There was a very fancy barn, air conditioned. Can you imagine air conditioning a barn where there weren't even any cows? We set up the dormitory in the barn and the boys had two beautiful weeks, swimming in a private lake, running wild in the private woods. It was wonderful for them. Russ was their hero, and he was our hero, too."

"He has a way about him, all right."

"Let me finish the story. The night before we were scheduled to pull up camp, the people who owned the estate returned." He laughed. "They had no idea that Russ had turned the place over to us. They knew Russ, but hadn't seen him in years. It was very embarrassing; the people were Presbyterians. They were ready to call the police, have Russ picked up and thrown into jail, have all of us evicted from the grounds. They went to inspect the damage that our little monsters had done. Of course they hadn't done any to speak of—a scarred tree or so from a treasure hunt. They went into the barn and saw the boys lined up fast asleep, looking like so many angels. Of course, they melted. That was five years ago and each year since, we've been invited back to the estate for our two-week summer camp."

"It sounds like Russ. He's all heart, Father, but very little head."

"That's the most important part, after all." He shook my hand. "I just had to tell that story to someone. Tell Russ, will you, that I was here. I don't think he knows that he established a camp for the orphanage. He'll laugh when you tell him, and be very pleased."

"Good night. It was nice of you to come."

"You look to me to be a man of guts and God, Mr. Maguire. Give the saints a hand, will you, in looking out for Russell Donnelly."

I started into the room where the coffin was, to see what progress Seguro's men had made. They were coming out as I went in and stood in line to pay their respects to the family. I went in and backed up the children, wishing I had brought my gun. I had forgotten it on the floor of Rourke's closet. When they neared Rourke, I stepped forward. They saw me, all right. They mumbled out of the corner of their mouths to each of the children and walked on. No trouble. I ducked out the other door and watched them from the reception hall. I wanted to make sure they left. This time they didn't see me right away. They stood in the jungle of people, then split up and circulated, pushing their way through the crowd. It was hard to watch both of them at once. I kept my eye on the man I knew. I lost the other one. I moved into the center of activity to keep tab on him. He weaved his way through the crowd without any direction; I stood as still as I could with people jostling me from every direction.

Maybe it's that I've been trained to have sensitivity to danger; the Army and the O.S.S. did that for me. Maybe it was just a sixth sense. But there was something different about the way somebody stopped behind me, an extra hesitation. Without even thinking, I wheeled around and caught his hand, which held a knife. I saw the glimmer of the sharp steel. I twisted hard and came up into his groin with my knee. The knife dropped to the floor and the man moved on to the front door. No one in the hall even saw what happened, it had happened so quickly. I stooped down, picked up the knife, and pocketed it. They were gone by then. I pushed my way through to the front door. They were walking toward a car waiting at the street. They had guts—I give them credit for that. Policemen were on duty at the front door and at the street, and these guys walked at a very normal pace. There was no point in stopping them. Again it would only be a scandal in the newspapers and even with these men locked up, there would be other men. Seguro had a big staff at his disposal.

In the butler's pantry, I turned on the big light and examined the weapon. It was a hell of a knife, beautiful steel, well-honed. It was long enough to go into the back and through the heart. I hid it in a cabinet under the sink. I'd come back for it later. It would be a great addition to my collection.

Russell caught me as I was helping myself to a glass of milk from the refrigerator. "Want a glass?"

"My stomach won't know what's happening to it." He took a glass from the shelf and I filled it for him. "We're in trouble, Maguire," he said.

"Now what?"

"Sylvia Newman," he answered. "I've been worried about her, worried about what she's up to. She doesn't figure; she doesn't make sense."

"Why not? Dough and power. What else is anyone after?"

"But it's more complicated than that. Mary, Forrester, Randy and I got to talking after you and Rourke left this afternoon. Incidentally, that was a hell of a thing for us to do. I mean we're not pretending any love for the old man, but even if it was a stranger lying down there we should have had more respect. We were in a mood, recreating happy times. I guess we lost control of our good taste. I want you to know I feel bad about it. I told Rourke I was sorry. I felt rotten about her. I have to remind myself sometimes that underneath all that high-level maneuvering of hers she really loved Father; her grief is deep and very real. She doesn't talk about it but I know how Rourke is, she feels things deeply."

He drained the glass and poured more milk. "Anyway, after you left, Forrester, Mary, Randy Lawrence and I had a talk. Forrester had most to say. The kid has some funny ideas, more than funny. Dangerous. Part of the Industries is connected with vital stuff. Steel, for example, uranium. It's all heavy industry. I didn't like the way Forrester talked. It was nothing I could put my finger on, precisely, but it had vague references here and there, pretty pink thinking. In my day it was fashionable to be pink politically, even dark pink, almost red. But today it means something else and has different consequences. Like I said, it was nothing definite the kid said. I mean he didn't advocate overthrowing the government and bombing the White House. It wasn't even like Forrester talking for himself; I had the feeling he was parroting what he had read or what someone else had told him. He didn't even use his own kind of language."

"Sylvia Newman," I said. That name was a magic answer for anything.

"I called a friend of mine in Washington. I got some information. It doesn't look good for Sylvia Newman."

"Rourke beat you to the punch. She already has a dossier on the girl. She has been associated with Communist-front organizations. But she works for the State Department. They must have cleared her."

Russ nodded. "They did clear her, gave her a clean bill of political health. I'm sure she's confessed her old mistakes to Forrester. She would have been stupid to hide her past from him, and she's not stupid, we all know that. But what Forrester doesn't know and what Sylvia doesn't know either is that she's about to get another going-over. They caught a man in Ithaca red-handed; a nice pipeline to Warsaw and through to Moscow. None of this has come out yet, they're still corralling information. But Sylvia's name has popped up a few times in his conversation. The guy turned canary. And his records don't mention her by name but there's a code number which seems to correspond to Sylvia's activities."

"That'll be nice. Maybe she'll be a Donnelly before the news gets out. Can't you just see those headlines."

"The problem is that I can't confront Sylvia with this. I mean I got this information from Washington strictly on the q.t. It's real hush-hush. If I tell Sylvia, she'll get word to her other cronies and the whole case could blow up. I mean it would be interfering with the FBI or something. I can't tell Forrester either because he'll sure as hell shoot his mouth off to Sylvia."

"Are you sure he isn't up to his neck in it with her?"

"No, Maguire. You're off the track. I know Sonny, I know how he thinks. This political thinking is new to him. I can see how he can go off the deep end on a thinking level. But this other business is … what would you call it, sabotage, spying? Whatever it is, Sonny isn't the type. I'll vouch for him all the way on that."

"I suppose you're right, but you can never be sure."

"How do we get rid of Sylvia, fast and neat? We can't have her name associated with ours once this thing breaks. Can't you just hear Rourke blow her stack? Holy cow! Listen, I believe Sonny should take over to represent the family, but I also have some sense about what could happen if he gets linked with Sylvia Newman and this case gets into the newspapers."

"Are you certain this information is accurate? I hate like hell to start playing cops and robbers on a fluke tip."

"The information came from high up, Maguire. I have good connections."

"Well, that leaves us with your plan, Russ. Which one of us is going to disillusion Forrester about his fiancée?"

"That's the answer, Maguire, the only way out. I've been thinking about it. Boy, I don't recognize myself with all the thinking I've been doing lately. The way I see it, it has to be you. You have to be the lover. This is going to be rough on Forrester; it'll hit him hard where it hurts the most. If I do it, he'll lose face all the way around. He'll walk out of here, right back to that school, right under all those books. He'll never come out. What we have to do is get him discouraged with Sylvia but not with himself, let him keep the confidence she has given him. That way, he'll be mad, disillusioned with her. It's going to make you a heel, but I'll rally to the cause, give him that old get-in-there-and-fight-'em routine. I can substitute for the backbone Sylvia is giving him until he functions under his own power. That way when he can take over the Industries, he'll want it even more. You've got to do it, Maguire. You've got to let Forrester catch you with her. It's got to be you."

"Does it have to be tonight? I'm pooped."

Russ gave me a smile of superiority. "I thought you were a craftsman at this."

"I have a certain craftsmanship, friend, but I also have only human endurance. I have been gone over today with blackjacks, guns and very recently a knife. Let me put it this way, I've had it for today."

"But you will do it?"

"It poses problems. What is Rourke going to say?"

"Rourke will understand. She'll be in favor of it. She hates Sylvia's guts."

I shook my head. "You have no romantic nature."

"Neither does Rourke, not where the Industries are concerned."

"The things I go through in the course of a day's work."

Russ licked his lips. "I wish it were me instead of you, Maguire. I hate to put you through this agony." He slapped me on the shoulder. "Lucky guy. I bet she'll be sensational."

"All of this on the premise that the lady will consent."

"I have nothing but confidence in you, Maguire. If you got through to Rourke, you'll make it with anyone. Say, I haven't asked you lately. Are you ready to tell me yet? How is Rourke, any good?"

"You shut your yap, Russ, and go back and make like a mourner. I'm going to make an investment in some vitamin pills and take it off my income tax as a business expense."

CHAPTER THIRTEEN

SLEPT all night.

CHAPTER FOURTEEN

T HIS WAS the morning of the funeral and all hell broke loose at the Forrester Mansion. It started off bad, right on the wrong beat. The butler awakened me with a summons from Rourke to appear at once in the library. I cut myself shaving, discovered I had spilled something on my tie, tried to take it out with water and made the spot three times as big. I called my office to talk to Tina and discovered she hadn't shown up for work yet, the explanation being that she had been to a political dance the night before with that punk Parsons and was well hung-over.

When I finally made it downstairs, the joint was jumping with flunkies from the undertaking establishment carting flowers and screaming at each other in hushed tones. Sylvia was in the middle of it all smoking a king-size cigarette through a Queen of Sheba cigarette holder. "You received the call to arms, too, I see." She blew smoke in my face. "Just by overhearing casual conversations I've counted five crises this morning."

"Where's Rourke?"

Sylvia shook her head. "Have no idea, lover. I consider it politic to stay out of her way today. You might try the parlor. There's been all sorts of goings on in the parlor."

"Thanks, love. You've been a bully help."

The parlor was worse bedlam than the hall. All the window shades had been pulled up, the draperies drawn back and sunshine flooded the room, a room accustomed to darkness. It's the way it is with a woman you thought was so beautiful and in the morning the sunlight floods her pillow and her make-up is

smeared and the wrinkles in her face show up and the imper-
fections in her skin. Two maids were on their hands and knees
scrubbing the floor. Flower arrangements were dismantled and
dead leaves and blossoms seemed to coat everything. The vacuum
cleaner was going over the furniture. A man on a high ladder was
changing bulbs in the chandelier. A maid was polishing a high,
ornate mirror. And in the center of it all, ignored by everyone, lay
the body of Carleton Donnelly, looking the worse for the wear of
the days of lying in state. Rourke was nowhere around. I started
to put down the lid on the coffin, looked at the dead face for a
minute. It was his face, and other faces. It was her face and it was
my face. It was Russ's face. In a way it was even Mary's face and
Forrester's face. You poor, dead bastard, I thought, rest in peace.

I found Rourke in the library on the telephone. She put her
hand over the mouthpiece. "Where the hell have you been? Close
the door." Then back into the instrument. "Let it drop another
point or two then start buying again. I'll call you later." She hung
up. "Have you seen the newspapers?"

"Haven't had time. I just opened my big, blue eyes. What
happened?"

"The newspapers are full of rumors. Rumors, rumors,
rumors. The substance is that from unimpeachable sources the
world has been let in on the secret, the Forrester Industries are
to be dissolved according to Carleton Donnelly's last will and
testament—dissolved, sold out any way possible. The *News* says
that Donnelly has definitely stated in the will that strength of
the Industries was his strength and that there is no one capable
of carrying on. The *Trib* has an interview with that brilliant
young tycoon of business and industry, one Dexter Cummings.
It is Mr. Cummings's expert opinion that the resources of the
Industries are unsalvageable, that he for one has no intention any
more of trying to buy up control. You know what all this means,
don't you?"

"It means that the stock is dropping a mile a minute."

"The ticker tape can't keep up with it. It's almost a panic."

"So what do you do now, coach?"

"You're such a bright one, Maguire, you tell me."

"Do I have authority to proceed?"

"You have authority to do nothing," she snapped. "If you have an idea, spill it."

"Listen to me, Red; there's only one way to stop this. If you want me to I can. Just say yes or no."

"I can't just say yes or no. How do I know what you're doing? How do *you* know what you're doing? This is disaster. You should hear this telephone. The Board has been in my eardrums since the six o'clock editions."

I rang for the butler. I did it with great authority, just like in the old movies on television. "Back in the old neighborhood we fight fire with fire."

"There's more bad news, if you want to hear it. Your dear friend Russell has disappeared. He didn't sleep in last night; no one has seen him. Vanished on the day of the funeral. That's going to make good copy."

The butler appeared. "You rang, madam?"

I wondered who was writing his copy. "No, I rang. I want you to do two things. First open the front door and let in all qualified newspaper reporters. No photographers. Just reporters. Make them show you a press card or something. Let them in one at a time, gang them all up in the hall and then march them in here. The minute you get them in here, go back to the kitchen and get me the biggest pot of the hottest blackest coffee you can find. Move fast."

When he was gone, Rourke said, "That's real bright. Now what? What are you going to tell them?"

"I'll tell them what I always tell everybody, the truth. It's a very simple thing to tell the truth. Everyone wants to know what gives. Now we'll tell them. Let Dexter Cummings know. Let everyone know. What the hell have you got to lose now?" I didn't wait for her to answer. I stuck my head out the library door and called out to Sylvia Newman, who couldn't hear my voice above the other confusion going on around her. I let out a wolf whistle and that did the trick. She turned around fast. "Where's Forrester?"

"What?"

I motioned to her to come closer. "Find Forrester and get him here within two seconds. Tell him to get his rear end in here and say nothing. Tell him to smile and agree with everything I say. Tell him to do precisely what I say or I'll beat his head in. Is that perfectly clear?"

"You *are* being masterful, this morning, aren't you, lover?"

I gave her a whack across her bottom. "No time for small talk, baby. Find him fast."

"Listen here, Maguire," Rourke was saying. "You can't just step in here and decide what to do. You have no experience in this. You don't know the vastness of this problem, the possible ramifications on an entire economy. You don't know the first thing…"

"One thing I know for sure; that Sylvia Newman broad has got to go. One way or another she has got to go."

"This all could have been avoided. Why did you have to open your face? If you had only let me walk into that lunch meeting yesterday and tell them that I was taking over. I knew this would happen." She stood up. "All right, Maguire, march the newspaper men in here. Go ahead. But I'll do the talking. I tell them the terms of my Father's will and I'll tell them that the children are unanimous in their decision. I am taking over. That'll do it. That will makes sense." She strode to the door, opened it wide. "Let them in. I'll take over."

I grabbed her arm, pulled her back. "You'll sit in that chair and keep your mouth shut. You won't say one word. You'll sit in that chair and look like a mourner. You'll look like a devoted daughter grieving for her father. You're no better than the other children; you're playing children's games, too, another kind of a game but still a game. You're beginning to hurt other people now. You know how many little stockholders are getting clobbered in this private feud between you and Dexter Cummings? Little people are getting hurt, money they thought was safe, and well-invested is being lost because you want to play King of the Hill. Nuts to that, Rourke. You're going to stop this, all of you. I have had a bellyful of the whole thing … all of you. I'm so sick of this mess I can't even remember that I love you. Tomorrow, when it's all over, I'll love you again, my teeth will itch for you and my stomach will do backflips. But that's tomorrow, Red. Right now, I'm going to make some sense out of all this."

Forrester broke in. "What's going on? They've let the reporters in. I won't have any statements made until we all …"

I grabbed him by the lapels. "I'm a little sick of you and your pious, historical approach. Did your lover girl give you my instructions? Did she tell you to get your ass in here and keep your mouth shut and a smile on your face? If she forgot to tell you, I'm telling you and I'm also telling you not to say one damn word. You nod and agree with whatever I say. Am I getting through to you?"

He tried to break away from my clutch. "What is this, Rourke? What's happening?" he asked.

"Maguire has flipped his lid." She threw up her hands. "We're all to blame. Maguire is drunk with power. He's all of a sudden decided he's Napoleon, a big Napoleon, a tall Hitler. When the reporters come in, deny whatever he says."

I held young Forrester tighter. "I swear to God if either of you opens your mouth, I'll slug you. That'll look great in the newspapers, too. You haven't enough sense to know what to do yourself and you're not decent enough to tell the truth, so I have to have sense for you, I have to have the decency you should have." I shoved him at the couch. "Now stay there and shut up."

Rourke had grabbed the phone. "I'll call the police."

I took the phone away from her and yanked it right out of the wall. I was feeling pretty strong until I realized it was only on a jack, but it made the right impression. Rourke gave up, leaned back in the chair, closed her eyes.

The gentlemen of the press entered single file, hats in hands, eyes surprised at being admitted into the inner sanctum of the Forrester Mansion. They lined up at the far end of the room into two rows, as if they were going to have their picture taken.

"My name is Maguire, gentlemen. I am a lawyer and I represent the children of Carleton Donnelly. They had no intention of making any statement of a business nature until a decent interval after their father's death. But your newspapers, by printing rumors and elaborating on rumors, have forced them to interrupt their days of mourning, to take time out on the day of the funeral when they have a right to solitude, to answer these ridiculous statements which your papers have been printing. They do not want all the small stockholders of the Forrester Industries to lose their savings and security. They feel that no grief can be so great that little people will be hurt as a result of it. That is the reason they are taking time out now, on the day they are going to bury their father, to tell the truth."

A voice from the back row said, "You're bringing tears to my eyes, Maguire."

And I said, "Watch out, buddy. I used to be CYO boxing champion. I'm a quick-tempered Irishman and I'm hot under the collar right this minute. If anybody else has any bright remarks say them now, while I still feel like clobbering somebody." There was an interval of coughing and fidgeting but no more bright sayings.

"Listen to me carefully. This is the truth about Carleton Donnelly's will. Get it straight and print it straight. Carleton Donnelly left all his money and all his holdings, including his stock in the Forrester Industries, to be divided equally among his four children. Each of the children gets one-fourth of the entire estate. Donnelly specifically stated that the children are to decide among them, and he specified *unanimously* decide, which one of them will represent the family's holdings in the Industries. On a very real level, it means they have to agree and decide which of them is going to take Donnelly's place as the director of the Industries. The will gives the children five days from his death to make their decision. I will tell you now that no decision has, as yet, been reached. The problem has not even been discussed. Their decision will be reached within the five days and a formal announcement made.

"The will stipulates that if they do not agree and do not arrive at a decision within five days, all holdings are to be liquidated and the money to go into the estate and then divided equally. I can tell you this much—the Donnelly children have no intention of letting that happen. When there is time to do it and that time is a decent time, they will make their decision and they will make it unanimously and the Forrester Industries will continue.

"There are no plans, no matter which one of them takes over the control, to change any of top level personnel of the Industries. The entire operation will proceed as it has been. There are no plans for selling out or cutting back. If anything, the great potential of the Forrester Industries will be expanded with the children owning the controlling block of stock. These are young people who want to see the business grow and they have the energy to encourage growth.

"That's the story. That's the true story."

I waited while pencils scratched.

"If you want another story," I continued, "you can tear apart the Dexter Cummings statement that he wants no part of the Forrester Industries now that Carleton Donnelly is dead. Do some detective work and see who's buying up the stock. You'll find that I have been buying up as much as I could in the name of the children of Carleton Donnelly. The other big blocks are being gobbled up under aliases and phony corporations by Dexter Cummings."

This statement caused a buzz and more pencil scratching.

"I want to ask a question." A meek man in the first row said this.

"No questions now. This has been enough of a strain for the family. You can ask questions when the formal statement is made. Now, you can all go."

Another voice from the back row. "Why aren't the other two here? How do we know you speak for all the children?"

"He speaks for me." I turned to the sound of the voice. It was Russell. He was tight, bleary-eyed and seedy-looking, but he was standing straight and that great head was held high. When the chips are down, the thoroughbred comes through. "And we can all assure you that he speaks for our sister, Mary, who is too upset to attend this meeting."

I waited for another voice to speak out, but they were quiet. "Now, gentlemen, get out of here and let them bury their father in peace." I stood back as they filed out. Both Rourke and Forrester were looking down, not wanting to cross eyes with any of the reporters. Even Russ held his ground, propped up by the paneled wall.

When the last man left and the door closed, Russ collapsed to the floor. We all ran over to him. He was all right, just unconscious from liquor. With the help of two men from the funeral parlor, Forrester led him upstairs. "Get him sobered up for the funeral," I warned. "The butler should have a pot of coffee ready by now. It's for me, but Russ needs it worse."

There were tears in Rourke's eyes and an expression I had never seen before.

"What's your problem, doll?"

She shook her head, tried to smile. "No problem. You, Maguire. You were like him, forceful, the way he was, and dynamic. It's the way Father handled a situation, straightforward, right from the shoulder. He was respected for it."

"Let's get this clear right now, Red. You're trying to make me something I am not, something I don't want to be. I am not your father. I am not like him. I didn't give out with that spiel to protect you or the other children. I did it for the reason I told those reporters; to stop little people from being hurt. You're building this up in your mind, trying to make me him or him me. I don't want any, Red. I want to be who I am. If you love me, love me for who I am, not because I remind you of him or because you're trying to re-create him in my body."

"I can't help comparing. I've always had to compare. There's never been anyone like him until you."

"It's no good that way. You have to love me for me, not for him."

"Isn't it enough that I love you," she said. "Must you dissect it? Nothing can live if you tear it apart, not even love."

Everything going on inside me was a signal that this was it, the big time for me, the time for loving and for being loved. It was there in my breathing, the way my heart beat, the way my senses came alive. "You know what you're saying, Red?"

She nodded without speaking.

"Then come out and say it, say it out loud."

"Maguire, I ..." She shook her head, denied the truth.

I said, "The hell with it, Red."

"No, not the hell with it. You can't expect me to change in a minute, be someone else with a snap of your fingers. When I say I love you, I destroy Rourke Donnelly. I destroy my dreams and I destroy my plans; the newspaper in Spokane, the uranium, the shopping centers, the oil maneuvers. All of that stops when I say I love you. I want both things, Maguire. I want you and I want my dream."

"The most important thing between a man and woman is love. If there is love everything else works out."

Rourke laughed then, throwing her head back, arching the wonderful line of her throat. "It's so easy for a man. Falling in love is so damn easy for a man. It doesn't change anything. His work is the same, his interests are the same, his identity is the same. But a woman becomes a wife, his wife, nothing else is supposed to be important. It doesn't cost a man anything to fall in love. He doesn't give up anything. A woman gives up everything to become *his* wife."

"You're not in love, Red. Face it. You can't be thinking what you're thinking and be in love."

"Don't be naive, Maguire. Don't try to fit everything into your tight little formula. I'm not Mary, killing time until I can get married. I'm not the girl in your office pounding a typewriter until some man frees her from that slavery. I'm who I am, just as you are. And what I am is exciting and challenging and powerful. It makes a difference, Maguire. You don't just junk all that. But it doesn't mean that you can't be in love. Everyone treats me like a machine, Miss Efficiency, Miss Do-it-all. All right, I am those things, I admit it, I'm not ashamed of it; I have had to be. But I am also a woman and I can be in love."

"It's not enough, Red. You don't love enough."

"It is enough. It's more than enough. It's enough to make me destroy myself. Isn't that enough for you?"

I tightened my hands on her arms. "Say it, Red."

"Stop it, Maguire; you're hurting me."

"Say it."

"I love you, Maguire."

And there it was, out in the open at last. Sure, I had forced it out of her, but left alone she would have withered away rather than say the words. And I knew the words were true. She was in my arms and she was shivering, limp. The only thing I can compare to it is when a fever breaks and you're hot and cold all at once, your energy is sapped and your body shakes. Then it's over and a cool calm comes, the crisis is over and pretty soon you sleep and when you wake again the mend begins. I was never so in love as I was at that moment. When her calm came, I kissed her. She looked at me again. "I love you, Maguire." Bells rang, drums beat, flowers bloomed, the moon was full and the sun was bright.

"Okay, Red. We know where we stand."

"I feel funny," she whispered. "Weak and strong, all at once."

I muzzled her hair. "Good sign. Your symptoms are perfect."

"You know what I'm going to do?" I shook my head. "I'm going to stop thinking. I'm going to let you think for me."

"The first thing I think is that you ought to wash your face. You're tears made a mess of your mascara and I raised hell with your lipstick."

"Do I look like an old hag already?"

"Sure. Go on. Get yourself back in condition."

She looked at her watch. "Holy cow! Do you know what time it is? We've got to get organized for the funeral. Let me go, Maguire. I have to fly." She tore out of the room, leaving the door open. Just as she came into the reception hall, the men were wheeling the closed casket through. The hearse was waiting at the side door again. The men stopped when they saw Rourke. She put her hand on the casket and lowered her head. She took a rose from the blanket of flowers covering the coffin. She cupped this one rose in her hand as tenderly as though it was a wounded bird. "All right," she said. "What are you waiting for? Get moving." The men wheeled the coffin past her. At the steps they had to lift it off the casters and carry it down. "Be careful. Watch what your doing! For God's sakes, don't you men know your business?" She looked around frantically. "Mr. Pritchard! Mr. Pritchard! Where the hell is Mr. Pritchard? He's supposed to be running this show; where is he?"

Poor Mr. Pritchard appeared from the parlor. "Yes, Miss Donnelly."

"I couldn't run my business the way you run yours, Mr. Pritchard. You're supposed to be in charge of this thing. Why aren't you supervising those men? They can hardly handle the coffin."

"I'm sorry, Miss Donnelly. They've made it all right." The casket was halfway into the hearse.

"Listen, there are some seating changes for the funeral. Get out your book and make notes, Mr. Pritchard. You're much too bewildered to remember anything." She waited. "You are to seat Mr. Maguire with me. Move my brother Russell over with my sister Mary and put Forrester on the other side of her. We will leave the chapel in that order. Mr. Maguire will accompany me and the other three will walk together."

"It is not usual, Miss Donnelly, for three persons to ..."

"I did not ask you what is usual, Mr. Pritchard. I am telling you the way it is going to be."

"What about Miss Newman? Mr. Forrester Donnelly has asked that Miss Newman be seated next to him and that he accompany her after the service."

"You will do as I direct, Mr. Pritchard. Miss Newman has no part of this. I am holding you personally responsible for seeing that Miss Newman, if she appears at the funeral at all, is seated nowhere near the family. Is that clear?"

"Yes, Miss Donnelly."

Sylvia Newman was descending the stairs during this last bit of conversation. This was a smart girl, even to dressing exactly right for each occasion. She was in plain black and wore a small black hat with a suggestion of veil. It was a costume of reverence to the dead which did not overstep the line into deep mourning. No matter what her politics, she was a hell of a good-looking woman, and she knew how to make an entrance. She even had Rourke stopped dead.

"Rourke, dear," she said, "I know how tight all our nerves are at a time like this. Forrester and I did talk this out quite thoroughly. I agree with you that only official members of the family should be together. But Forrester says he can't go through the ordeal of the funeral alone, not without me. Poor dear, he is so much more upset than he appears. I finally agreed that his feelings are more important than decorum. Even if people talk, it won't be for long. They'll all soon know about Forrester and me."

"Miss Newman, I will sign the check which will pay Mr. Pritchard. As long as I am in charge, Mr. Pritchard will follow my instructions."

"There would be much more gossip, Rourke, dear, if Forrester sat in the back with me, away from his family. It will make people think there is a schism which, of course, would be deceiving and particularly disturbing in view of the announcement Mr. Maguire made to the press. If people thought there were family differences…"

"Forrester wouldn't do that, Miss Newman, not even for you. I may underestimate the extent of his grief, but you underestimate the extent of his family loyalty."

"I have a marvelous idea, Rourke," Sylvia went on. "Why doesn't Forrester sit with you and I'll sit someplace in the back with Mr. Maguire. After all, Mr. Maguire and I are two of a kind here, both in the same position."

Rourke turned around to look at me. I guess I was smiling. "Mr. Pritchard, did you find out the protocol? Who proceeds whom, the Senator or the Governor?"

"The Governor, Miss Donnelly. I checked it with the *Tribune*."

"That's dandy. Make sure you get it right." She started up the stairs.

"What about Miss Newman?"

Rourke kept walking. "You have my instructions, Mr. Pritchard."

"Rourke," Sylvia called. Rourke stopped without turning. Sylvia Newman said, "Forrester will guarantee the cost of the funeral. If necessary he'll pay for the whole thing out of his share just for the comfort of having me next to him."

"Maguire," she called, "I've stopped thinking. You think." She ran up, out of sight.

Sylvia Newman slinked up to me at the library doorway. "Yes, lover. Think. What do you think?"

"I think you look lovely."

"That's usually a good way to soften up a lady. But it won't work with me, lover."

"I think you'd better do as Rourke says."

"Forrester will never consent. He has his heart set on my being at his side."

"I'll convince him," I said. "I have a choice. I could say 'Sylvia doesn't want to hurt your feelings; she knows how much you want and need her but she feels that it would be improper for her to sit with you'."

"You make me sound like such a dear."

"Or I could tell him the truth. I could tell him that if you show up as a member of the family, the newspapers are going to wonder who you are, they might even be ingenious enough to find out. They might even dig deep enough to find the records of the inquiry the State Department had before they hired you."

"Forrester knows all about that. I was given a clean security slate."

"Sure, doll, I know all about that. But I think Forrester would agree with me that there could be possible misinterpretations by the press. After you're married and Forrester is all set up with what he wants, there won't be any danger. But now, at this particular time, I'm sure he'll agree with me that a badly slanted news story at this time would not only hurt his chances of representing the family in the Forrester Industries but it would hurt the Industries themselves. You know how the average newspaper reader is—he jumps to conclusions. You show him pink and right away he sees red. I think there's too much at stake for you and Forrester to risk this. Don't you?"

"Bless your blackmailing little heart."

"Which way will it be? What do you want me to tell him?"

"Neither, lover. I'll tell him myself that I think I ought to stay in the background for a while."

"Good girl." I patted her shoulder.

She patted my shoulder back. "Bastard," she said.

We smiled at each other and I went upstairs to whip Russell into shape for the funeral.

I poured some coffee into the cup by Russ's bed, and drank it. "How do you feel?"

"Like a tiger." He held his head. "I was out of practice."

"What happened? How come you fell off the wagon? You were going so well."

"It's a long story and not very pretty. What a mess of a man I am." He rolled over, buried his face in the pillow.

"You're out of character, aren't you, Russ? I didn't figure you as being sorry for yourself. I don't dig this self-pity bit. It's out of context."

"The trouble is that I'm out of context at home. Usually I'm surrounded by people who don't mean anything to me. It's easy to be without conscience when no one means anything to you. Why wasn't I in Timbuktu when this happened? Why wasn't I somewhere where you couldn't find me?"

The coffee was cold but I drank it anyway. "You'd better pull yourself together, Russ. The forces are forming for the funeral."

"I'm not going. I've thought it all over, looked at it from every angle, drunk and sober. I have no right to be at the funeral, no moral right. They say love and hate are different expressions of the same thing. But it doesn't matter. I hated him, and he hated me. Maybe what we both did was love each other too much, were too disappointed in each other. What the hell. I'm on record as hating him and he's on record as hating me. Why be a hypocrite? I'm going back in character. Let the papers print the story tomorrow: Donnelly heir gets soused in saloon while father is buried. That's what everyone expects; that's us, that's the way we are. It wouldn't be honest to do anything else. You're the vice-president in charge of honesty around here. Admit, buddy, the only honest thing for me to do is get stewed while they bury him."

"Okay, I admit it. Now what?"

"Now, I go out and get loaded again."

I drained the coffee cup, stood up, started to leave. "Have fun, Russ. Happy landing."

"Hey! Wait up, Maguire."

"What do you want?"

"How come you're not trying to stop me. What the hell kind of watchdog are you?"

"I agree with you, Russ. You'd be right in character, living up to your press, being the guy you think you are. I'm not playing God to anyone, Russ, not for any price. You do what you think best."

"I like you, Maguire."

I grinned. "I like you, too."

"Want to know why I got loaded last night?"

"You're dying to tell me. Go ahead."

"It was Mary, poor little Mary. She was all mixed up about love again. It was your fault. You had your chance with her. Last night it was my turn." He stood up on his bed, blew dust off the Yale pennant hanging on the wall. "It was pretty much of a nightmare, Maguire. I'm not the man of iron you are. I never felt so sorry for anyone in my whole life. She was begging to be a woman. I got the pitch about being only half of the same blood. She reminded me of some stuff when we were kids … kid stuff. The whole routine; I got it all, everything, the tears and the panting."

"Poor Mary. She ought to get married fast."

"You think I didn't touch her, don't you? Do you think I'm like you, no heart, no feeling for how someone else feels? I'm not made like that." He sat down on the bed again, his knees pulled up under his chin. "I'm a damn chameleon. I'm what other people want me to be. I'm all things to all people and nothing to myself." He shook his head. "If only I had been in Timbuktu."

"You weren't. You were here, and you came willingly. No one forced you."

"Why don't you ask me? Why don't you ask me about Mary, what I did?"

I shook my head. "I don't have to ask, Russ. I know you; I know what you are. You have something a guy like me can never have. You have class, and breeding. All my life I've scoffed at class and breeding. I couldn't afford to believe in it. Let's face it, my father was a bricklayer and my mother was a washwoman. That's it, right there. Nothing wrong with it, nothing wrong with them. They were honest, and I'm honest. My morals are better than yours; in a lot of ways I'm smarter than you. I've certainly made more out of the raw material of my life than you have. But you have class, and you have breeding."

Russ snorted. "You fraud. You phony. You've fallen, hook, line and sinker. We've taken you in with our big house and fancy ways. I thought you were smarter than that. Class and breeding—that's a laugh. Look at us, look at how we behave, look at what we are. Class and breeding. You're a jerk, Maguire. You're like all the boys from the wrong side of the tracks. You think dough and mansions and big cars mean class and breeding."

"No, I don't, Russ. I know what it really means. It means that when the chips are down, you behave like a thoroughbred. I know damn well you didn't lay a hand on Mary. And I know that at the last minute, when they bury your father, you'll be there with your family where you belong. You can't help it, Russ. It's bred into you. You can't be any other way."

"Hey, Maguire."

"What?"

"I came that close." He measured with his fingers. "In my mind I was that close." He held his fingers higher so that I could see how close he had come. "That's why I got loaded. I was ashamed of myself, for what I was thinking, frightened at how weak I could be. It was awful, Maguire. I couldn't stay in bed after that. I tried and I just tortured myself with my own thoughts. I had to get out. It was a question of a cat house or a saloon. I came to a saloon first."

"Like I said, when the chips are down ..."

"Another thing, Maguire."

"What?"

"See if Sonny has an extra black tie. I ought to wear a black tie to the funeral."

"Sure thing, Russ."

Forrester had finished dressing. He was at the mirror squeezing a pimple on his face.

"Russ wants to know if you have an extra black tie?"

"I have a dark blue one. It looks almost black. I'll take it to him. Is he all right?"

"He'll make it."

"I hear you're sitting with Rourke."

"Any objections?"

"No, none at all. I wish Sylvia would sit with me. She's so sensitive about things. She wants to make sure that she doesn't do anything to intrude on the family. I've never known a sweeter person than Sylvia. Honest, John, she's about the best there is. I told her it would be all right, that you were sitting with us, but she said she wouldn't feel right about it." The pimple was bleeding; he dabbed at it with a Kleenex. "I'm a lucky guy, luckier than I ever thought I could be."

Rourke stormed into the room, all dressed. She, too, was in black. Her hat had no veil, none of the standard trappings of mourning. "Where the hell is Mary? I can't find Mary. We have to be downstairs and ready to go in fifteen minutes. She's not in her room and she's nowhere."

"I haven't seen her."

"Neither have I," Forrester said. He made a final dab with the Kleenex, took the tie for Russ. "I'll ask Russ, maybe he'll know."

"What do you suppose she's done this time, Maguire? It's ridiculous. She knows the schedule as well as any of us. It probably has something to do with that damn Randy Lawrence. Try to find her, please. I'm in a terrible mess. I've just found out that the governor of Colorado and the governor of Oregon have flown in for the funeral. This means a general reshuffling of governors. The only thing worse that could happen now is if the President showed up. Where the hell would I put him?"

"I wouldn't worry about it. He wasn't a great admirer of your father."

"That doesn't matter. He loves going to funerals. He'll probably show up just to make sure Father is really dead."

"I'll try to find Mary."

Randy Lawrence was asleep, his head cradled in the crook of Mary's arm. Mary made no attempt to cover her nakedness. She put her finger to her lips so that I wouldn't talk, wouldn't disturb her sleeping prince. They were in the storeroom behind the playroom on the third floor. I didn't have to look hard to find them. This was inevitable. They had made a bed out of an old mattress and pillows of old draperies.

"You have ten minutes to get dressed and be down in the reception hall. The funeral procession starts there, and it starts promptly."

Lawrence opened his eyes, took a few seconds to realize the situation he was in, made a gallant effort to cover up Mary with his own body. "Relax, buddy. I've seen broads before. Get your pants on and get Mary downstairs and make it fast."

"Let me explain, Maguire," he said.

"You don't have to explain to Johnny, honey. He understands." Mary had that bovine expression of satisfaction. She must have worn Lawrence out. He had trouble getting to his bare feet and staying steady on them.

"I have no comment on this," I said. "If it's what you want to do, it's no skin off my nose. If anyone finds out about it, one of you will have told, not I. I'm interested in only one thing. Get downstairs and make it fast."

In the hall, I whispered to Russ, "I didn't think Gingiss had that many funeral suits for rent." The board of directors were all in striped pants and oxford-gray coats and light-gray gloves. They were the honorary pallbearers. They stood closest to the front door, two abreast, like a small army of pigeons. Directly behind them, Mr. Pritchard was apologetically arranging Governors and Senators who were following the hearse to the chapel. The rest of the dignitaries were going directly to the services. Next came us, the family. Forrester was fidgeting with his tie, Russ was hanging on to me, Rourke was talking to a secretary who made notes in shorthand. Mary had just come down and was straightening the seams on her stockings, generally pulling herself together. The smile on her face was engraved there; it would never come off. Sylvia Newman had made herself scarce and Randy Lawrence was still upstairs. Behind us were the servants, dressed in their Sunday best. The contingent was formed; it was time. Mr. Pritchard's platoon of sad men opened the front doors and the parade started into the blaze of midday sun. Never in my life had I seen so many black, chauffeur-driven Cadillacs in one place. Lake Shore Drive was blocked off by rows of policemen. The sidelines were crowded with spectators and photographers. And this line of Cadillacs ran all the way from across the drive up the driveway of the Forrester Mansion and through the backyard. As we neared the front door, Rourke put her arm through mine, bent her head down. She whispered back to Mary. "For God's sake, don't trip," and we stepped out and began the long walk to the family's limousine.

I muttered to Rourke. "If I had known all this was going on I would have invited all my old boyhood friends from the CYO."

"Shut up!"

I bent my head like everyone else and followed the pack. I felt a little guilty when I realized I was enjoying this. I have to admit it, I liked the whole thing. I had felt sure of myself when I gave the statement to the reporters and was puffed up because they seemed to respect my position as well as what I said. I liked the idea of Rourke's being in love with me. More and more I found little thoughts sneaking into my mind, ideas about running the Forrester Industries. Secret pictures flashed into my consciousness: Maguire, the giant of Industry. I remembered about the man I knew who had won the Horatio Alger award, but he hadn't married his success, so that daydream I rejected. I even found myself making logical explanations about why it wasn't so bad to marry wealth and power. I convinced myself that the Donnelly clan needed me to save themselves. The closer I got to the Cadillacs the more grandiose my rationalizations became. I had saved part of the American economy. I had protected the little people, the small stockholders. I had a duty to them to take over and make sure they weren't caught in the squeeze. With every step I was growing greater in my own mind. If the line had been any longer, I might have been President of the United States.

As I was helping Rourke into the car, I heard someone say, "Well, I'll be—" I looked up and it was a policeman on a motorcycle, his mouth hanging open in surprise. It wasn't just any policeman, it was Harry Callahan. Harry is a first cousin on my father's side, not even once removed.

CHAPTER FIFTEEN

Russell said, "And here we are."

"I wish they had buried him in the ground rather than in that crypt in the mausoleum. There's something so final about being buried in the ground. I mean the way a mausoleum is, everybody is just put on a shelf, the way you'd file something away." Mary unlaced Russ's shoe, took it off, and rubbed his foot. "When I die I don't want to be buried in the family mausoleum. I want to be buried in the ground, and I want flowers to grow over me, pink flowers, and I want a lilac bush near my head."

Rourke had a headache. She was massaging her forehead. "Shut up, Mary. I've had enough of death and dying."

Russell said, "And here we are."

We were there, all right, back at the old stand in the library, everyone resuming his former position, me in my corner, Rourke in her father's leather chair, Russ supine on the sofa, Mary curled up on the floor near him and young Forrester in the lounge chair. We had already been through the bit with Russ turning on the light over his stepmother's portrait. All the small talk had been made about the personalities at the funeral. Everything was exhausted but the real issue, the family decision on the control of the Forrester Industries. Rourke and I had discussed nothing further; we had no plan of action, no time-plot to spring on the other children. My idea was to wait it out, let things follow a normal course of action. Forrester and Rourke would have to ram each other head-on and reach a stalemate. Then was the time to suggest the compromise, step in and tell them about Rourke and me, offer myself as a middle ground, and answer for everybody.

Randy Lawrence came into the library, "Hi," he said. He sat near Mary, looked from one to the other, got no reaction from any of us. I had to smile at the way Mary was handling herself. She was as aloof to him as the others, she was that sure of her new power as a woman. "It was an awfully nice service. My father said, leave it to Rourke to run a good show. It was clever to have the leaders of three different religions speak."

"It wasn't clever," Mary snapped. "They wanted to. They asked to be permitted to speak. Our father was an important man in the world, Randy. We didn't ask them, they asked us. Isn't that right, Rourke?"

"Shut up, Mary. I have a headache." Russ touched Mary's hair, offering comfort and protection.

"Listen," Randy began, "I know this is an awkward time for all of you. I seemed to have gotten myself in a middle position, I have my father and Dexter pushing me from one side. And there's my … well, my loyalty and my feeling for you on the other side."

"You don't owe us anything, Randy," Mary said. "You owe no loyalty to us."

"What's the matter with you, Mary? What are you sore at?" Randy was the wounded little boy, confused by this change of Mary's attitude.

"I'm not sore. I'm just saying you have no loyalty to us. You don't owe us anything. Not us … not me. You don't owe me anything just because you were nice to me."

"Nice to you? What are you talking about, nice to you? Is that what you think I've been? Doesn't it mean any more to you than that?"

Rourke ran her hands through her hair. "Why don't you two have a lovers' quarrel somewhere else?"

Young Lawrence stood up, walked over to Rourke. "What I have to say concerns you, mostly, Rourke. Dexter Cummings is waiting outside in the hall. He wants to talk to all of you. It's a business deal. I made him promise to wait until I could talk to you first."

"Tell him to get the hell out of here." Rourke said it without emotion. She was tired, worn out, and, I suppose, sad.

"Give him a chance, Rourke," Lawrence pleaded. "It can't hurt anything to listen to him."

"My father kicked Dexter Cummings out of this house years ago. He hasn't been admitted here since, and it's sheer temerity for him to be here now. Go back and tell your Uncle Dexter to get out. Tell him I said so."

Forrester stood up. "I think we ought to listen to him, Rourke. I don't see what harm it can do. After all, this was a fight between you and Father against Dexter. It has nothing to do with the rest of us. Dex is a big stockholder in the Industries. He has a right to talk to us. We're not sacrosanct."

Rourke jumped up, stood face to face against Forrester, as tall as he. "What right have you to suddenly reappear on the family scene and think you can take over? You want to be a big man, don't you, Sonny? You think it's just great to take over, step into Father's shoes. What right have you? You're a stranger here. You haven't been around for years. It was your choice; no one forced you. You're a stranger, Sonny. You're a stranger to all of us. Blood is a thin tie."

"We've been through this before, Rourke."

"You're damn right we've been through it before. And we'll go through it again and again until you get it through that medieval brain of yours that you don't belong here, that it's too late to take out citizenship as a Donnelly."

"And we've discussed that before, too. You know you drove me away from my own house, kept me away. I guess I ought to realize the truth about you, Rourke. I guess I ought to listen to what people say."

"What *people* say, or what your friend Miss Newman says."

"All right, it's what Sylvia says about you. I haven't listened to her up till now. I alibied for you; I've tried to explain everything to her, tell her what a rough life you've had. You *are* my sister, you know. No matter what, I have that feeling for you."

"I'm touched, Sonny. But I have something to tell you. I feel nothing for you. Nothing. You're no more related to me than a piece of wood or a hunk of stone. I feel nothing for you. Do you understand that? Nothing."

I would have stepped in, but Russ beat me to the punch. He put his arm around his younger brother and in a gentle way led him back out of Rourke's fire. "This is never going to get us anywhere. We all know that. We're all who we are and who we're going to be. Nothing ever changes. This could be ten years ago, twenty years ago. Same thing. It could be ten years from now. Same thing. What's the point of it, what's the point of fighting it. Give up. Why don't we all give up?"

"That's your way, Russ. Give up, give up, run off with a slut movie star. Live it up in a saloon. Never be a man, never face anything the way a man does, make decisions the way a man has to. That's your life," Rourke said. "But it's not mine."

Randy Lawrence said, "What shall I tell Dexter?"

"Tell him," Rourke answered, "to get out and stay out."

"If Rourke won't talk to him, Randy, the rest of us will." Forrester looked from Russ to Mary. "We'll talk to him, won't we?"

Russell turned to me. "What gives, Maguire? What do we do now?"

"It's the same thing," I explained. "Either you all talk to him or no one talks to him. And there you are back at the heart of your problem. All of you against Rourke. Rourke against all of you. Russ, you pegged it right on the button. This is what your father wanted, this is why the will was written. He planned this battle very carefully. He knew it had to take place. But he didn't rig it; that's the interesting part. He didn't set it up so that Rourke would have to win. I'm sure he wanted Rourke to win, but he depended on her guts and her cunning; he left Rourke her own resources to beat you down."

Russ lay down again. "Nice speech, Counselor. But like I said, what do we do now? Do we talk to Dex or don't we?"

"Do you all agree to do what I say?" I waited for answers. No one rushed to give me his proxy.

"Listen, I have no right here," Randy Lawrence said. "And I'm in the middle, between you and Dex. But I know Dex; I know how he operates, how tough he can be. You think I'm a jerk, don't you, Rourke? Maybe I am. I don't want any of the things you want. I want to take Mary away, marry her and live happily ever after. I'm that simple a guy. But as simple as I am, I know that you're all destroying each other now. By fighting and arguing you're playing right into Dexter's hands. In my opinion you have to talk to him, but Maguire is right, you all have to talk to him and be together when you talk to him. If Maguire is here to speak for you, let him do his job. I'll give you this tip—Dexter has new respect for Maguire. He sees Maguire as something formidable now, not just a bunch of muscles acting as a family bodyguard. I think Maguire can handle Dex."

Forrester said, "I'm willing to do what Maguire says."

Mary stood up and moved next to young Lawrence and took his hand. "I say let Randy talk for us. He's going to be a member of the family. Let him talk for us."

Lawrence shook his head. "Not me. I'm not going at it with Dexter. I told you I didn't want any part of this, I don't want the power and I don't want the glory. I don't want any responsibility. We talked this out this morning, Mary. Everything I said still goes. What about you? Do you still feel the same?"

She didn't have to answer, it was all there in her eyes—love for her master.

"I say let Johnny make the decision," Randy said.

I called to Russ. "What about you?'

"Okay, Counselor."

"All right. Talk to Dexter Cummings. Let him talk to you. See what he has to say. There will be time then to make decisions," I said.

Rourke said, "What about me? Don't I get to vote for you, Mr. Maguire? Doesn't it have to be unanimous that we agree to abide by your decisions?"

"I thought it went without saying, Red."

"Did you?"

"You said this morning that..."

"This is this afternoon, Maguire. I'm still running the show, and don't forget it. Don't any of you forget it. You're lost without me, all of you. I'm the only one who knows anything about the Industries, how to run them. I *am* running them. I *am* the Forrester Industries. Without me they'd collapse. Remember that, all of you." She walked quickly to the door and flung it open. "Dexter. Dexter Cummings. Come on in," she said.

Rourke and Dexter shook hands. There was no one in the room for him but Rourke. They looked good together, they went well together. Seeing Rourke again had thrown him off guard; I could tell that. He had underestimated the depth of his feeling for her. Seeing her again brought it all back in sharp focus and it caught him off balance. But not Rourke. Not Rourke. She was straight and sure of herself, in command from the moment he walked in the room. "You look well, Dexter. You keep yourself fit. The gray hair is very becoming."

"You're the same, Rourke. Just the same."

"Of course I am. What did you think, I'd wither and die on the vine? Spinsters look different these days, Dex. They don't shrivel up and wear black ribbons around their necks. Old maids aren't what they used to be."

"I'm sorry about your father, Rourke. I know what he meant to you, how important he was to you."

She turned her back on him, walked to the fireplace. "That's very sporting, Dex, very old-school tie. Now that you've made your niceties, make your deal."

He looked around, taking his time, slowly regaining his composure. "I have many memories of this room. Good ones, bad ones. All the children have grown up. Russ, I'm glad to see you. I've missed you."

"Hello, Dex. Long, long time."

He nodded at Mary, said her name. He shook hands with Forrester and came up to me. "You're quite a boy, Maguire. Cloak and dagger. Brains. That's where I miscalculated. I didn't figure you for brains. Your friend Eddie Seguro is real mad at you, Maguire. It's out of my hands now. It's a personal grudge with him. He's out to get you. He wants blood. You made him look like a punk, and he's mad."

"I can take care of myself."

Cummings nodded. "I'm sure you can. You take real good care of yourself." He turned to the others. "You may not know this, but I offered Maguire a hundred thousand dollars to tell me the contents of your father's will. I would have gone higher if necessary. But it was no deal. I liked you for that, Maguire. I liked you because you were honest. Then you spilled the whole thing to the newspapers. You said for free what I could have paid hard cash for. Then I realized that you're smart enough to know that what I offered you was chicken feed compared to what you can get by playing it smart with the Donnelly clan."

"Say what you have to say, Cummings. Make it complete, because when you're through I'm going to slug you." I was mad.

Rourke was impatient. "Start talking, Dexter."

"I admit everything you think about me, Rourke. I want control of your business. I want to be head of the Forrester Industries. It's that simple. I've tried everything. I've tilted the market, bought stock cheap. Maguire put a halt to that. Did you see what Forrester closed at? It's halfway back to where it was before your father died. I tried strong-arm tactics. Maguire shows the scars of that. I even tried Randy here, but he got smart, decided to become a family man—a Donnelly family man—and play his cards on the other side. I'm at the end of my rope. I come to you now prepared to buy you out, straight business, no tricks, no mumbo-jumbo. I need thirty-two thousand shares to gain control. I'll buy them at ten dollars per share over the market price as of the day before your father died. It's a good deal for you. If you refuse, I'll know I'm beat. So I'll unload all my stock—and I have plenty to unload. You know what that will do to the market; nothing can stop the bottom from falling out. I know you have enough dough to stand the gaff, but it will be rough for you. Your stock will be worth a fraction of what it's worth now. You'll have to pay taxes on the value of the stock when you inherited it. You won't be ruined, you have too much money for that, but it'll be tough for you. On the other hand if you sold me thirty-two thousand shares at eighty-six dollars a share, that's a lot of money."

"Dexter doesn't understand our problem," Rourke said. "Dexter doesn't understand about Sonny. You wouldn't know Sonny, Dex. He's become a big man. Sonny wants to be Chairman of the Board. He wants to put in big innovations in the Industries, let the unions in where they haven't been able to get in so far. He wants to put in a profit-sharing plan for the employees, increase the retirement plan. I think his eventual plan is to turn over the ownership of the Industries to the employees. He has lots of plans, Dex. Big plans."

"Rourke can be pretty cruel, Dexter," Forrester said. She's trying to make me seem a fool. I know what I want. I know I can be good for the Industries."

Cummings wasn't having any. "You *are* a fool, Forrester. If you want to run the Industries you start at the bottom. You do what your father did. You think he walked into this house and laid down the law to old Simon Forrester? Do you think he tried to threaten the old man? Not on your life. Carleton Donnelly went to work in the steel mills. He sweated it out there. Then he worked at the lumber camp. Each business in turn saw Carleton Donnelly starting at the bottom, working up. He didn't steal control from old Forrester by threatening or saying 'Look what a good boy I am.' He fought for control. He knew the Industries inside and out. He knew everything there was to know, how to make it better, how to make more money. Your grandfather Forrester knew damn well that Carleton Donnelly had to control the Industries. Donnelly knew more than the old man; he had more ambition, more ideas. The Industries needed Donnelly to grow and to flourish. Your grandfather knew that. He was beat out by superior knowledge and ability. If you want to run the show do what Rourke did, find out what makes the businesses work. Rourke found out the hard way, too. Summer jobs at the mill, inspections of the mines. She isn't just a well-dressed lady boss. Rourke is like your father; she knows what she's doing because she's had her hands in it, seen it on every level. This isn't something you learn from a book, and wishing won't make you fit for it.

"I'll make you a deal, Forrester," Cummings went on. "Turn the voting power of your stock over to me; that will give me control. You go to work in the Industries, learn it the hard way. When you show evidence you know what you're doing, you can take over."

Young Forrester didn't say anything. His pimples were bright red, and he nervously flexed his fingers back and forth. Rourke applauded and laughed.

"Well," Cummings asked, "is it a deal?"

"You don't understand, Dex," Forrester said. "I don't expect you to understand. Your way is the old way. My way is the new way. There are men who are trained experts. They can feed me information. My job is to take that information and put it together, run it from an executive capacity, direct everything toward the most good for the most people."

"That's great. Experts feed you information. How will you know what the information is about, how will you know if it's accurate? Don't be stupid, Forrester. I'm giving you what you want. It may be twenty years away, but when you get it you'll know how to handle it."

"No deal," Forrester said. "You don't understand."

"All right, what about all of you?" He faced the children. "You've heard my proposition. Thirty-two thousand shares at eight-six, The alternative is that I unload and let the bottom fall out. Which will it be?"

Mary said, "Why are we fighting it? At last we have a chance to get some money, I mean money we can call our own. Why should we risk all that just because Rourke and Sonny want the same thing. I don't think either of them is fit for it. I think Dexter knows what he's doing. He talks the way Father used to talk. I think we should sell."

Dexter said, "Good for you, Mary. You talk sense. What about you, Russ?"

"I don't know, Dex. It doesn't matter very much to me. I've just been thinking. I'm going to make a picture in Hollywood. It doesn't matter very much to me."

"Talk sense to them, Maguire." Cummings wheeled around. "You turned down a fortune from me, gambled on getting a bigger fortune from them. If they don't take my deal there won't be any money left for you."

I said, "Are you through with this guy, Rourke? I'm ready to slug him now."

"One minute, Maguire. Dex, you came here to play with children. They're children, but I'm not. Your threats mean nothing. You can't afford to dump your stock and let the market drop on it. You'd be wiped out overnight. You've hocked everything you own to buy up as much stock as you have. Every holding of yours is mortgaged to the teeth, even your house and your cars. You owe every friend and every business associate you know. You're not fooling me, not for one minute. You can't destroy us. If you try, you'll destroy yourself and everyone connected with you. Even your dear brother-in-law. It's a bluff. Blindman's bluff, a children's game. Now slug him, Maguire. Slug him twice, once for me."

I hit him. I hit him hard and I hit him twice, once for me, once for her. He lay on the floor rubbing his face. "Get him out of here, Randy," I said. "Get him out." Randy went over to help him up, but Cummings pushed him away, stood up under his own power, and, with what dignity he had left, made his exit.

Rourke said, "Now has anybody else any bright ideas?"

"It's a stalemate, Rourke," young Forrester said. "We're nowhere."

"We just have to agree," Mary said. "It'll be just awful unless we can agree. You heard what Dexter said, the market price will drop on the stock. We won't be able to get very much for it. We've just *got* to agree."

It was wonderful to watch Rourke move, to manipulate her hands; even the way she carried her head was a beautiful thing to see. She had the advantage now, and she understood how to handle it with an animal kind of instinct, the closing in for the kill. "Obviously, you're both right. We have reached a stalemate and we cannot afford a stalemate. This kind of problem always occurs in business. There had to be a compromise. I'll have to give and you'll have to give. If neither gives, we all wind up zero. If we both give a little, perhaps it can be worked out so we all get what we want."

"That makes sense," Forrester said. "What's your deal?"

"Since we cannot agree on which one of us will represent the family, let's get an outsider, an unrelated person who will look after all our interests." Rourke walked back to me and put her hand on my shoulder. "We've all relied on Maguire through this. I think we've all come to trust his judgment. He hasn't taken sides on this, you against me or me against you. He'd done what he thinks is the honest thing; he's acted for all our interests. Let's have Maguire represent us. Sonny, you want to be in on the act. Okay. But some of what Dexter Cummings said was true. You can't step into this job without and background of actual experience. I have the experience, you have the desire, and Maguire has the faculty of doing the right thing at the right time. The three of us can work together. If we fight on policy, Sonny—and I'm sure we will—Maguire can referee. He can make us see each other's point of view."

Forrester said, "This is not settling anything, Rourke. This is a delaying action. I know what you're thinking, you think given enough time, you can wear me down, beat me out." He shook his head. "This time you're wrong. I admit that Dexter is right; you need practical experience, you need to know what you're dealing with. So I'll start at the bottom and learn. I'm not afraid of that and I'm not afraid that I'll get lost or disheartened on the way up. You forget one big difference with me now. Rourke—I have Sylvia. I have all the things Sylvia means to me. When I falter, she'll be there. I'm not alone any more, and it makes a difference. I have something to work for. I'll take the deal because I have courage now. I'm not afraid anymore." He turned to Mary. "Is it all right with you, Mary? Will you settle for Maguire as a compromise?'

Mary looked at Randy Lawrence. "I guess so. I like Maguire. He's honest. I trust him. I trust him, don't you, Randy?"

"It seems like the only answer," Lawrence replied. "What's the legal technicality? The will says that you will decide which one of you will take over. It doesn't give you the specific option of selecting an outsider to represent you."

Rourke dismissed this with a wave of her hand. "A technicality we can cope with later. It doesn't matter. Well, we're agreed, then?"

Russell stood. "What happened to me? Don't I get a vote?"

"I'm sorry, Russ. I just assumed you'd go along if Sonny and Mary agreed." Rourke left my side and went over to him. "What do you say?"

"What gives with you and Maguire, Red? What is it with you two? Is it love, or business, or mad passion? Or is it all three? I'd like to know what it is with you two."

"It doesn't matter, Russ," she said.

"It matters a lot, Red. I like Maguire, and I love you. You're my sister. What's going to happen? Are you and Maguire going to get married and live happily ever after? Or is it a straight business relationship? Or are you going to keep him at arm's length panting for you, giving him just enough to keep him interested but not enough so that he'll possess you enough to make his own decisions. I think what you two are to each other has a great deal to do with this."

"Maybe you're right, Russ." Rourke looked from him to me. "Do you want to tell them, Maguire, or shall I?"

"Let me tell them, Red, and you listen, too. I've had it; up to my ears, I've had it. I don't want any more." I looked at Rourke, seeing the surprise in her eyes. Maybe it was more than surprise, there could have been hurt there too. "Forrester is right. A compromise is a delaying action. It doesn't solve anything; it puts everything off to a later date. Maybe that's the right thing to do. I think it is the only solution for you at this point. But you've got the wrong boy. I'm not having any. For three days I've been in the middle of this, caught up in your lives. You've taken me and torn me apart, you've made me be something else to each one of you until I don't remember who I really am. I don't want to spend the rest of my life being a referee and nursemaid to the Donnelly children. There isn't enough dough in the whole world for that. None of you is going to change. I can see that now. For a while I liked the idea of playing God. I felt important. But I wasn't playing God; I was just fuel for the same old family arguments you've been having since you were born. I was one more person to be thrown in the ring and be devoured by the Donnelly lions. You can't see this the way I can. You can't have the perspective I have now. But you all enjoy this—this is the way you live, fighting with each other, standing up to or shying away from each other. You'll never change, not one of you. You don't want to, really. You're trying to put me on a permanent retainer fee to be the scapegoat, to be sacrificed to the lions. And none of this changes any of you or affects you at all. It's just the lamb who gets chewed up, the blood sucked out of it, the good meat eaten up and gristle spit out. Not me, kids. I'm no lamb. Chew up somebody else. Leave me alone." I started to walk out on them. "You know, one at a time, under other circumstances, it might have worked out. I could be a good friend to you, Russ. We understand each other. I could have played big brother to Mary and Forrester. I could have married you, Red, and loved you and lived happily ever after. But not all of you at once, not all of you being what you are to each other. I'm sorry, but I'm getting out now while I'm still in one piece."

Russell applauded to break the silence which followed my farewell address. "I have new faith," he said. "And I have new respect for you, Maguire. You are the man I thought you were."

Rourke said my name, and the way she said it could have meant a lot of things. Maybe it did mean a lot of things. It sounded like love and it was a sound I wanted, but not this way. And tomorrow I'd begin to feel the hurt and each day I would feel it, some days less and some days more, and there would be the time when it would only hurt occasionally. Keeping it a secret from myself, I would begin to search again, the inevitable search as inescapable as the force of gravity, the rotation of the earth ... a woman you love, the whole damn Philharmonic playing background music, the sun and the moon shining at once, bright flowers blooming in pristine snow. A man has to keep looking.

Upstairs the door to Sylvia Newman's Chinese Room was open and everywhere there were symbols of disorder. She had flown the coop. On the dresser the newspapers were spread out. The headlines gave the answer. SEEK MYSTERY WOMAN IN SPY QUIZ. There was her picture and the picture of the Russian whose mistress she was. It was all spilled, everything which could destroy young Forrester, his new strength and his new courage. Maybe Rourke did it, maybe Russ. Probably Russ. He must have known I would never have seduced Sylvia Newman under the prescribed conditions. It didn't matter who did the destruction, it had to be. Everything had to be. Rourke had to win control of the Industries. She was destined; Carleton Donnelly had destined her. And back to the archives and the protection of history books for poor Forrester. That was predestined too. He had had a taste of the outside world, enough so that he would want to hurry back to the cloister of learning, to lick his wounds and rebuild his shell. And Russ? He would go on until the alcohol ate away his liver or somebody's yacht sank or an airplane exploded. Only Mary had a chance. Poor Mary. She had a chance.

And me. I went back to my room, packed the shreds of my belongings. I checked my watch. It wasn't yet five o'clock. I dialed my office. Tina answered the phone. "Mr. Maguire's office."

"Is it now? Well, this is Mr. Maguire."

"Not the famous Mr. Maguire! Not the darling of the rich folk who saved the Forrester stock from crumbling, not the champion of the little investor. It couldn't be *that* Mr. Maguire."

"You're right. It isn't that Mr. Maguire. It's the Mr. Maguire you used to know. How long ago? Only four days."

"Three days. I remember distinctly. Three days ago I spent a long evening making Hungarian goulash. I'll never forget it."

"What did you ever do with all that goulash?"

"I froze it. For a while I was tempted to throw it out, but I got cold feet and dumped it in a bag and threw it in the freezer."

"How long will it take to thaw?"

"A few hours," she said. "In time for dinner tonight."

"What about you, Tina?"

"What about me?"

"How long will it take you to thaw?"

She was silent for a minute and then she said, "I'll be ready before the goulash."

THE END